"This is a strong, tough no— ... itability that seasons the g—...
—John D. MacDonald, author of *The House Guests*

"One of those rare books with the blood of reality rushing through it."
—Martin Cruz Smith, author of *Polar Star* and *Red Square*

"FAUST WRITES OF NATURE AND MEN LIKE HEMINGWAY, with simplicity and absolute dominance of prose skills."
—Bill Granger, award-winning author of *Hemingway's Notebook* and *The November Man*

"Inevitably, RON FAUST WILL BE COMPARED TO HEMINGWAY."
—Robert Bloch, author of *Psycho*

"THERE'S A RAW UNDERCURRENT OF POWER TO FAUST'S WRITING."
—Adam Hall, award-winning author of *Quiller*

"You can't read a book by Ron Faust without the phrase 'MAJOR MOTION PICTURE' coming to mind. With each book Faust finds a new way to grab you by the short hairs and shake you into fresh self-discovery. You may shudder, but YOU'LL LOVE IT."
—Dean Ing, *The New York Times* bestselling author of *The Ransom of Black Stealth One*

"HEMINGWAY IS ALIVE AND WELL AND WRITING UNDER THE NAME RON FAUST."
—E. J. Gorman, author of *The Marilyn Tapes*

Also by Ron Faust

Fugitive Moon
In the Forest of the Night
When She Was Bad

The Burning Sky

Ron Faust

A TOM DOHERTY ASSOCIATES BOOK

NEW YORK

This is a work of fiction. All the characters and events portrayed in this book are fictitious, and any resemblance to real people or events is purely coincidental.

THE BURNING SKY

Copyright © 1978 by Ron Faust

Cover art by Tim Jacobus

A Forge® Book
Published by Tom Doherty Associates, Inc.
175 Fifth Avenue
New York, NY 10010

Forge® is a registered trademark of Tom Doherty Associates, Inc.

ISBN: 0-812-53532-4

First Forge edition: June 1995

Printed in the United States of America

0 9 8 7 6 5 4 3 2 1

For Gayl

One

*B*en was telling the Texan about the cats.

There were four cats left, he said: two fine adult mountain lions, a male and a female, that he had trapped near Chama; an immature jaguar that he had smuggled across the Mexican border—"tranquilized so deep with Sucostrin I thought I'd killed her"—and a big, amber-eyed goddamned *leopard* that he'd bought from a small roadside zoo east of Gallup. He'd read in an Albuquerque newspaper about the outfit going bankrupt and had driven down to see if he could buy any of their cats at a good price. They had a mangy old lion, a living rug; a diseased mountain lion; an ocelot—"all apathetic, not paranoid like real cats"—and the leopard. The leopard was half starved then, wormy and diarrheic, but even so you could see that it was a magnificent animal, a cat of cats, a god of cats.

They were sitting in the ranch-house living room. The Texan did not seem to be listening.

"Mr. Stuart," Ben said, "I've medicated and fattened that cat and his fur and eyes shine like the moon now. He stares at you and the hair stiffens on your neck and arms. You know he can't get out of the cage, but still you can hardly breathe because of fear. That cat is so smooth—he moves like yellow oil, he just flows, and he makes all the other cats I've seen look like plaster knickknacks."

The Texan looked at his hands. "Did that roadside zoo use the leopard in any kind of animal act?"

"No sir, that cat never jumped through a hoop. He was just exhibited."

"How much money do you want, Ben?"

"Sixty-five hundred."

"That sounds high."

"The leopard is an endangered species."

"It still sounds high. Awful high."

"Hell, the pelt alone is worth a lot of money these days. And I'll probably lose some dogs."

"It still sounds high, Ben." That slurred Texan drawl: the men spoke monotonally, the women whined up and down the scale.

"How much do you think it would cost me in fines if the State Game and Fish Department catches me running these illegal hunts?"

"Six five zero zero," the Texan said softly, and he shook his head. "I don't know."

"Okay, I'll keep the leopard."

"Is it really that much cat?"

"He is."

"How much for the cougars?"

"Twenty-five hundred for the female, three thousand for the male."

"I expect my wife will kill the male."

"Fine."

"But I want to see the cats before it's a deal."

"Of course."

"How much for the jaguar?"

"Forty-five hundred."

"You said the jaguar wasn't mature."

"She's almost full grown. All right, four thousand dollars."

"My son will kill the jaguar."

Ben nodded.

"We haven't got a deal yet. I have to see the cats."

"Certainly."

"If I like the cats we'll kill three of them. Maybe all four."

Ben was annoyed by the way the Texan discussed the hunts; killing was the object, of course, but ideally it should be regarded as a kind of rite, a blood ritual, performed with awe and fear and sacrifice— the sacrifice of a little pride at least. But Stuart talked about destroying those magnificent cats as if he intended to put on a leather apron and go outside to butcher hogs. Gratuitously killing something so perfect had to diminish you unless you approached the act with humility. If you could not see that then the whole business began to resemble murder.

"I might kill one of the cats with an arrow," Stuart said.

"Fine," Ben said. "But not the leopard."

"Why not the leopard?"

"It would be too dangerous."

The Texan stared at him.

"Take one of the mountain lions with your bow and arrows. Or the jaguar."

"Ben," Stuart said quietly.

"That leopard would eat us up."

"Ben, if I pay out sixty-five hundred dollars for the leopard I'll by God kill him any way I please."

"No."

"I'll kick him to death if I want to, if I pay for him."

"I haven't sold him yet."

"But you will, won't you, Ben?"

"Maybe I'll give him to a zoo."

Stuart smiled, nodded. "You're broke, aren't you?"

"No," Ben lied.

"You are so, Ben, or you'd be running cattle instead of cats."

Ben shrugged. "These are bad times to raise cattle."

"I know." Stuart polished the right toe of his cowboy boot on the back of his left pant leg. "I hope we can get along, Ben."

Ben watched him.

"You're involved in a couple of lawsuits, aren't you?"

"I'll win."

"Maybe, but lawsuits are expensive to fight."

"Look, Mr. Stuart, leopards are—"

"Call me Tom."

"—much too dangerous to fool with. They're crazy. They're absolutely pure cat, the boiled-down essence of cat. Kill the jaguar with an arrow. Hell, the jaguar is nearly as big."

"But it's a jaguar."

"No, I just can't permit it."

"Let's see, three thousand dollars for the male cougar, four thousand for the jaguar, sixty-five hundred for the leopard—that's thirteen thousand and five hundred dollars. Am I right?"

"Sounds right." Ben waited.

"That's a lot of money."

"I can use it." The lawsuits, taxes—federal, state, and county—and all the debts . . . Christ yes, I can use it.

"Think it over, Ben."

"You'll have to use your rifle on the leopard."

The Texan glanced at his watch. "My wife and boy should get back from town soon. We can pack up and head back to Dallas."

"I'll find other hunters."

"Will you, Ben? It's late October. Do you think you can find hunters who'll buy three of your cats before winter? Can you make it through the winter without my money?"

"I'll sell a piece of my land."

"I don't believe you *can* sell any of your property until the lawsuits are adjudicated. And even if you could, the IRS would claim the money."

"Listen, how do you know all of this?"

"Ben, among other things, I'm an officer of a bank. Bankers like to know the financial status of the folks they deal with."

"Shit," Ben said.

"What do you think, Ben?"

"There's nothing to think about."

"You're a stubborn man."

"So are you."

Stuart nodded. "Stubbornness is expensive. I have the resources now to be stubborn, but I can recall days when I couldn't afford the luxury."

He arose and began walking slowly around the perimeter of the room. Ben saw his house through the Texan's eyes: a sprawling collection of nine variously sized and shaped rooms, built room by room as needed over more than one hundred and forty years without any kind of unifying plan; the out-of-plumb adobe walls with the plaster cracked at points of stress and the crumbly dirt and straw showing through; the warped, slanting hardwood floors (you could drop a ball at the northwest corner of the big living room and it would roll diagonally to the southeast corner); the soot-blackened walls above the two adobe Indian fireplaces; the low ceilings supported by heavy, age-darkened *vigas*.

Stuart circled the room, pausing to look at the Navajo Two Gray Hills rugs, Hopi kachina dolls, Pueblo Indian pottery, the *santos* and *retablos*, the Penitente *muerto* doll in a wooden cart, flintlock rifles, the rotting conquistador's saddle, stone arrowheads and axes, fetishes. Sometimes, when Ben had a gullible client, he claimed that the saddle had belonged to Coronado himself, and one of the muskets to Kit Carson. But he didn't think it would be smart to try to con this Texan, who obviously was a tough, no-crap kind of guy. The artifacts no longer belonged to Ben; he had sort of pawned them to a friend when things started going wrong with the ranch and he'd never raised enough money to buy them back. Now he sometimes borrowed them in order to impress a client with local color. He had an interesting lie for every object.

"What's this?" Stuart asked.

"An old scalp," Ben said. "My grandfather took it off a Ute brave." A safe lie. It really was a scalp, but Ben had bought it from a Taos Pueblo wino (who might have stolen it from a kiva), along with a peyote pipe, a leather pouch, and three stone fetishes.

"Okay," Stuart said, nodding. "All right." He approved, but of what?

"The Utes were great fighters," Ben said.

"Were they?"

"Everyone feared them—the Pueblos, the Navajos, even the Apaches."

"My grandaddy took a Comanche scalp when he was a young man," Stuart said.

He moved slowly, Texas-macho style, as if each step and gesture had been precisely choreographed. Stuart was a big man, about six four, heavy-bellied, with reddish hair and a rusty gunfighter's moustache and gray eyes that faded into silver around the pupil rims. He was a country boy who had made it big in the city. He lived in Dallas, but he wore a big white Stetson and a gray Western-cut suit and three-hundred-dollar ebony-colored cowboy boots. Ben watched him, thinking that the frontier styles and frontier ethics lingered in the air-conditioned banks and offices of metropolitan Texas. It seemed that most male Texans were secretly prepared for a trail drive or a gunfight.

Stuart turned away from the scalp. "I saw some buffalo on the way into your place."

"I have a small herd."

"How many?"

"It varies—I sell a couple off every year. I have eleven now."

"Why do you keep buffalo?"

"I don't know. I like them around, They don't require much care, they're pretty much on their own."

"Are they wild, then?"

"Wild enough so that I stay clear of the bulls."

"I'd like to shoot one."

"That would be all right."

"The biggest one in the herd."

"Okay."

"How much?"

"Eight hundred dollars."

"Ben, you've got more than a little bandit in you."

"I can get that much by selling one for market."

"I don't want the meat, just the head and hide."

"Three hundred dollars, then. I'll keep some of the meat and sell the rest."

"What other game do you have around here?"

"Come back in three weeks and I can promise you a mule deer and a big black bear that I've been keeping track of. And maybe an elk. It'll be the season then and all legal game."

"Do you worry about the game seasons, Ben?"

"You bet. My fees go up with the worry."

"I'm not interested in deer or black bear. I've killed real bear—polar, Kodiak, grizzly."

"Do you like bird hunting? We can poach some grouse or wild turkey."

Stuart waved his hand in the direction of the mountains. "Are there any bighorn sheep up there?"

"A few. Eighteen or twenty, maybe."

"Well?"

"They're transplants. The native stock was shot out a long time ago."

"So, Ben?"

"So I'd hate to kill a ram before the herd has really taken hold."

"How much?"

"Let me think about it. They're up high, twelve thousand feet, and sometimes hard to locate. It might take days to get one."

Stuart nodded. He seemed to become bigger, heavier, slower as the moments passed. "It looks like fair pronghorn antelope country to the west."

"It isn't."

"No antelope?"

"Well, there are some around Tres Piedras."

"But none around here?"

"Well, yeah, a few maybe." Ben sometimes saw antelope around the salt blocks he put out for the buffalo and the few steers he still raised, but he regarded them as shy pets, rare and sadly beautiful creatures who ran as you run in your best dreams, and who soared over fences with the ease of angels. There were only nine antelope left in the herd, down from last year's thirteen, and he didn't want Stuart to shoot any of them. The antelope were special. Ben loved the pronghorns more than any other animal; they were valuable in a way he could not explain to himself. He had the feeling that he had unconsciously made some kind of bargain with the antelope.

"Could we take one of them?" Stuart asked.

"Kill one?"

"Of course kill one," Stuart said, smiling faintly.

"I don't know." Ben thought. If I can keep my land then the antelope will continue to have a place. They can't live in a housing development or on the grounds of a shopping center. If I sacrifice one of them . . . "Yeah," he said, "I suppose we could try for an antelope."

"How much?"

"A thousand dollars."

"Jesus Christ!" Stuart said softly, savagely.

"That's fair."

"Fair, huh, Ben?"

"One thousand dollars," Ben said.

"Fair! Listen, I went on a complete safari to Africa in 1968 for just about what you want to charge me for a few cage-deadened cats, a tame buffalo, and a seventy-pound antelope."

"It's not the season. We'd have to poach. It's open country where you find antelope—we might be seen."

"One thousand dollars. Bleeding Jesus!"

"Take it or leave it," Ben said.

"Screw the rich Texan, huh, Ben?"

It was after midnight now, the Stuart family had gone to their rooms, and Ben sat at the desk in his office-bedroom and reviewed his debts: the bank, the bank again, once more the bank, federal and state and county taxes, old grain bills, physician and law-yer and veterinarian and mortician fees, employee salaries—he had not paid Mrs. Jaramillo or Bernard for months. Stuart was a bullying crud, but his money would help. God, would it help. First, Ben thought, I'd pay off the taxes, and then I would be free to sell the strip of land along the highway, and with that money . . .

Now Ben added the cost of an antelope to the column, and he noticed that he touched the pencil lead to his tongue before writing, as his father had done. That irritated him. His father had been nearly illiterate, and he'd used writing implements (and the telephone and TV and motor vehicles) as if they were alive and hostile. Ben was aware that he had recently adopted his father's habit of shrugging with one shoulder, and sometimes he hummed on final consonants, like his father, and he licked pencil lead and shouted into the telephone and stood hipshot in the fields and stared toward the west, where the good and bad weather usually originated.

Benjamin Pearce, Sr., had died three years ago. The funeral had been icy and simple. There were no words, no ceremony. No one wept. Hawks circled in the transparent turquoise sky. You could see dust funnels far out on the desert. Fifty yards away a colony of prairie dogs, erect and still, watched in a kind of parody of respect. The old man had been buried in the small family cemetery beneath the grove of cottonwood trees. Ben had given his father the funeral he'd asked for. "Bury me like a dog, Ben," he had said while he stank of cancer and his eyes oozed a cloudy mucoid substance. That was during the final days, when his mattress had to be covered with plastic and his sheets burned each morning because they'd been fouled by blood and excrement. "Dogs have a good life. If they can't eat it or screw it they piss on it. Bury me like a dog."

"Okay."

"I mean it now, Ben."

"I know."

"I've never been ashamed until now."

"There's no reason for shame."

"I'm dying in my own shit and blood. Just throw me into a hole in the ground."

Ben switched off the desk lamp. After a while his eyes adjusted to the darkness, and through the north window he could see the Big Dipper and Polaris. Now, in darkness, the room seemed to smell of his father: leather, sweat, livestock, old age, sickness and death.

Ben had not felt much over his father's death: a small sorrow, a low-frequency pain, but nothing like grief, and no pity. Pity was not an emotion the old man would have appreciated. He had been empty of pity, for others and for himself.

He had been a lean, thick-boned, silent man who always appeared angry. He looked furious even when he laughed; especially when he laughed. His only pleasure was work. He didn't drink more than once or twice a year, did not smoke, gamble, gossip, read, listen to music, dance—he worked. Maybe work was an anesthetic. He might have been born burned-out, or burned himself out in youth. He was an honest man, though. He was honest and he built things, but there seemed to be a secret fury for destruction even in his building.

He was eighty years old when he died. He had been bored for at least the last fifty. He and his father,

Ben's grandfather, had together defeated their big piece of nature, and there was really nothing more to do: no more trees to cut down, no more streams to divert, no more grasslands to use up, few predators remaining to shoot or poison. The pioneer should move on when his job is finished. He should go north or farther west and start over again, because he is a man who is incapable of living happily in the country he has changed. What mysterious dread and guilt they must feel, Ben thought, because they have to love the land more than they hate it, and love it only as it was when they first saw it. Others can order the destruction of a mountain or river or forest and feel less remorse afterward than a child who has killed his first songbird. But Ben's father and grandfather had not been that sort of criminal. They were of the old breed, and though they used the land up to the point of destruction, Ben liked to believe that they did so out of ignorance, confusion, and that they at least felt a little pain afterward.

They were arrogant, Ben thought. Not half as arrogant as the modern-times destroyer who occupies walnut-paneled offices high in concrete-and-glass towers, but arrogant enough. His father had died while owning a lot of land, and he had been a rich man for a time, and he had believed that he was rich because he was virtuous. Anyone could do it, he'd say during the rich years, if they're not afraid of sweat.

"That's horseshit," Ben would say. Sweat is the cheapest commodity of all; you can hire unlimited sweat for a bed and bread and beans.

"My pa and me paid for all of this in sweat," the old man would say.

"You did no such thing," Ben would reply. The money came out of grassy fields, gone to sage and cactus now; and from timber, half a mountain of pine and fir; and from water, snow that melted in the high country and entered his land clear and cold; and from mineral, a small pocket of silver formed eons ago; and from the hot summer sun and autumn molds. Sweat was incidental.

Ben knew that he was like his father in many ways. He wished that his father had been a better man, so that he might have become a better man.

Now he lay down on the bed and looked up through the skylight. Moonlight frosted the glass, pooled against the crosshatch of frames, and a billion miles beyond he could see the familiar cold machinery of the constellations. Ben had slept better before he put in the skylight. There was something about the nightly exposure to infinity that made him restless. He often awakened during the late hours with a feeling of vertigo, a sensation of slowly spinning off toward a black-rimmed sun.

Two

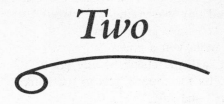

*B*en went into the kitchen early the next morning and found Mrs. Jaramillo, his cook-housekeeper, sitting hunched over the table and deeply inhaling the steam from a cup of black coffee. Her dentures were on the table, and when he entered the room she twisted in her chair, turning away, and inserted them. Anita Jaramillo was a bulky, lantern-jawed woman in her middle sixties. She had worked for the Pearce family since she was thirteen.

Ben poured a cup of coffee, sweetened it with sugar and condensed milk, then sat down at the table.

"We don't have any eggs," she said. She spoke with a slight lisp because of her poorly fitting dentures, and with a faint Spanish accent.

"That's okay," Ben said. "I'll just have cinnamon toast."

"We're out of bread. And cinnamon."

"Cereal?"

"We're out of everything, Benny."

"Okay, why don't you take the old Dodge into town and buy everything we'll need."

"Do you have any money?"

"I'll write you a check."

"Ben, will the check be any good?"

"Yes, by the time it gets to the bank."

"Sure," she said.

"I'll get a down payment from Stuart today. As soon as he sees those cats he'll be glad to give me half of the money."

"Well, I'll pay for the groceries and then you can pay me back."

"Thanks, 'Nita, I appreciate it."

"Benny, what the hell—if you go under you take me with you. What are those *Tejanos* like?"

"What can I tell you?"

"Just smile, huh, Benny?"

"Right, we'll both smile for a few days and then they'll be gone."

"What do you want me to buy at the store?"

"Get some good cuts of meat, steaks, a roast, chops. And let's feed them some of the local foods, they'll probably like that. Posole, chili, sopaipillas, piñon nut candy. Do we have any chokecherry wine left?"

"Two gallons."

"Buy more wine at the store, red and white. Get some decent stuff, not the acid we drink ourselves. And get beer, and some booze. I don't know what they drink—Scotch and Dr Pepper, probably. Get a jug each of Scotch, bourbon, gin and vodka. And some mixes. Fruit, too."

"This going to be expensive."

"They're paying a lot of money, 'Nita. If they eat good and drink good maybe they'll feel good. What's the matter, don't you have enough money for all the stuff we need?"

"I got enough."

"I'll pay you back this afternoon."

"Get some money from him today, Benny. Don't let him stall."

"I'll get half."

"Cash his check right away. Have the bank in town call his bank in Texas. Get the money."

"There's no need to worry. He's rich."

"That's what worries me."

Ben finished his coffee and went outside. He stared out across the desert. The sun had not yet risen above the mountains, and it was cold; his breath smoked, there was frost on the ground, and thin shells of ice had formed over puddles in the yard. It was a misty blue morning, a dream dawn, the day after the day after Creation. The sky was luminous and seemed to hum, or rather was somehow the visual equivalent of a humming sound. If you stared at it for a long time you got the impression that it was not a single color but billions of shifting dots of indigo and cerulean and cobalt and pale aqua greens—a vibrating pointillist sky. Snow dusted the shoulders of the higher mountains. The desert rolled off to the west, was interrupted by the jagged dark gash of the Rio Grande Gorge, passed on, and then far away erupted into buttes and mesas and blue-smoke mountains.

Ben was surprised to see Mrs. Stuart down near the grove of cottonwoods, her hands on her hips. He started toward her.

She turned.

"Good morning," he said. "You're up early."

"I didn't sleep well."

"It might be because of the altitude. We're at more than seven thousand feet here."

"No," she said. She turned and stared over the desert. "Smell the morning."

Cold, piñon-wood smoke, sage, chamisa, desert herbs, rotting apples and apricots from the orchard. Half a dozen ravens cawed high in the branches of a yellow-leafed cottonwood.

"The sky here is amazing," she said.

"Isn't it."

"It's actually turquoise this morning. Dark blue turquoise in the center and green turquoise on the horizon."

"The Indians call turquoise the 'sky stone.' "

"Do they?"

"And a writer once said that this sky was beautiful and horrible."

"Who said that? Lawrence?"

"No, Aldous Huxley."

"Really? Horrible?" She looked at him. Her expression was grave, but he had the feeling that she was secretly laughing at him. "Do you see horror there?"

He smiled. "No," he lied. "Do you?"

"Oh, yes, absolutely. The horror is there."

There were moments when Ben saw something horrible not only in the sky but in the entire landscape. At times, when he was fatigued or depressed, the sky and desert and mountains didn't look like anything more than an abstraction of harshly angular wedges of space and color, geometry, but without the comfort of limits—it didn't end, it went on and on, encysting one in space as a fly is trapped in amber.

She was staring intently at him. He believed that she had intuited the lie.

"Well, sometimes . . ." he said.

She was a very good-looking woman a few years younger than Ben, thirty-six or thirty-seven. Her eyes were large, slightly tilted, and so deep a blue that in a certain light they appeared black. Today she wore an impractical riding outfit (Neiman-Marcus, Ben supposed), suede leather jodhpurs tucked inside high boots, a silver concho belt, a beige blouse, and a suede gaucho-style jacket. Her long blond hair was tied into a ponytail by a strip of coral-colored ribbon. She spoke with a soft drawl, but without the whining intonation of so may Texas women. A honeyed, whispery voice.

"I walked through the little graveyard over there," she said. "Was that all right?"

"Of course." He looked toward the cleared space beneath the cottonwoods: an iron-spear fence with an unhinged gate, weeds, leaves, small headstones, and crooked, pastel-colored wooden crosses.

"Who is buried there?"

"My family mostly."

"I saw the Pearce name, and I saw Romeros and Santistevans and Mondragons and Valerios, too."

"Some employees of my grandfather and father are buried there."

"There are plastic flowers on some of the graves."

Ben nodded.

"Do you put out the plastic flowers?"

"No. Relatives of the dead come here once or twice a year. Why do you ask?"

"I wondered. It's vulgar. Plastic flowers on a grave are in bad taste, don't you think?"

Ben was silent for a time. "I don't know," he said. "They were put on the graves out of honest emotion. Wouldn't you say that bad taste is usually the result of either excessive emotion or insufficient emotion?"

She smiled. It was the first time he had seen her smile. "Oh," she said. "I'll have to think about that."

They stood quietly, and then she said, "Are the cats beautiful?"

"Yes."

"How beautiful?"

"Just beautiful."

"Describe them."

"Well, I don't know, they have cold yellow eyes, and the ends of their tails hook when they lash them. They smell strong, cat smell, and they stare directly into your eyes the way cats will."

"You like them, don't you?"

"Yes."

"Then why do you do this?"

He shrugged.

"Tell me, I want to know."

"To keep this ranch. To keep condominiums off that little cemetery over there. The last year I sent a herd of cattle to market I lost forty dollars a head. Forty dollars a head, seven hundred head—figure it out. Now I'm just trying to get by. Last year I gave some of my land away to squatters just to get it off the tax rolls, and when I can I'll sell some of my property along the highway to the development types. I'm trying to get by."

"But surely there must be a better way."

"I haven't found it."

"These hunts are a stupid way to earn money."

Ben nodded.

"And you can't earn very much, either."

"More than I would working on a construction gang or as a cowboy."

"I believe you like it. Where are the animals now?"

"About four miles from here, up in the mountains."

"And they're beautiful?"

He shifted his weight, looked away from her.

"And they smell strong, they stink?"

"Well, yes, but they've been caged."

"Their eyes are cold and yellow," she said. Was she mocking him? "The ends of their tails hook when they lash them."

"Have you hunted much?" he asked.

"No, never."

"Never?"

"I've shot skeet and trap, but I've never killed anything."

"But you are going to kill one of the cats."

"I know."

"Why now?"

"Tom wants me to."

"He does? Why?"

"I don't know, really. But it seems to mean something to him."

"Do you think you'll like the killing part?"

"I don't know. How will I know until I've done it?"

"Then you think you may like it?"

"I may."

"And you may hate it?"

"Yes."

"But now you have no idea of how it will make you feel?"

"No, how could I? I haven't *done* it yet." And then she said, "Wait, here comes Peter." As if they were discussing something her son should not hear.

Peter walked toward them. He was a lanky, awkward boy of fifteen or sixteen. He wore his long brown hair in a sort of Dutch-boy style. His skin was a waxy grayish-white. Peter had his mother's small bones and delicate features, and his father's meaty, big-knuckled hands. The hands did not appear to belong to his body, and he seemed alternately ashamed and proud of them, concealing them most of the time, but occasionally showing them off, watching in a kind of objective wonder as they formed into huge fists or sliced the air in karate chops. Ben thought he was a troubled boy, too serious, too sickly, and much too young for his years. He was tall, nearly six feet, but his voice was still flutey (when it did not crackle with asthma), his cheeks were as smooth and hairless as a baby's, and there was no breadth to his shoulders. From certain angles he looked like a pretty girl.

Now he joined them, stepping between his mother and Ben.

"Hello, dear," Mrs. Stuart said. "Is your father up yet?"

"Yes," the boy said. "He wants you."

"He does? Why, Peter?"

"I don't know. He can't find something, I guess."

"Is he angry?"

"A little. You know."

"Isn't it a beautiful morning, Peter?"

He nodded.

"Well, all right," she said. "I'll go see what the bad old gorilla wants." She turned and started toward the house.

"Morning," the boy said softly, shyly.

"Good morning, Peter."

"I heard some coyotes last night."

"Did you?"

"They sounded close, just outside the house. The dogs set up an awful racket. There must have been twenty coyotes out there."

"Two coyotes can sound like twenty."

"Is that an eagle, Mr. Pearce?"

"Where?"

Peter pointed to the sky above the desert where a hawk was riding an early morning thermal, effortlessly rising in a corkscrew motion.

"No, that's a hawk."

"Are there eagles around here?"

"Some, yes."

"You know, I'd really like to have a hang-glider. My father said he'd buy me one, but my mother is against it. If I had a hang-glider I could fly like that hawk."

"That sure would be something."

"I think I would be afraid at first."

"Who wouldn't?"

"But a friend of mine who has a Rogallo kite says that the higher you go the less fear you have. He says when you're up high it's like flying in a dream. The fear goes. He says it's free and dreamy and you don't want to ever come down."

"Well, maybe when you're a little older."

The boy was silent for a time. He did not seem to know what to do with his body; he changed positions, shifted his feet, folded and unfolded his arms, stuck his hands in his back pockets and then withdrew them.

"I would be afraid though, at first."

"So would I, Peter."

Another silence. "Are the cats big, Mr. Pearce?"

"They're big for their types, Peter. They aren't as big as lions or tigers, of course, but they're good-sized."

"Are they dangerous?"

"They can be. Just like one of your hang-gliders can be dangerous."

"But not the mountain lions," he said. And then he confidentially added, "I'm a little worried about my mother. I don't think she'll be good at hunting."

"Any big cat can be dangerous."

"I've read where mountain lions never attack people."

"That's wrong."

"Jesus," the boy said. "And I'll bet a jaguar is worse than a mountain lion."

"Look, Peter, my dogs will distract the cats. And

I'll be there with a shotgun. These hunts will be a lot safer than your automobile ride from Dallas."

"Listen, what do you think about this, Mr. Pearce?"

"About what?"

"About all of this Masai crap of making a man out of me by having me kill that jaguar."

"Is that what your parents think?"

"Just my father."

"Well, it's stupid."

"Right, right," he said, scuffing the toe of his shoe in the dust. "Oh, man, if you only knew."

"Don't you want to kill the jaguar, Peter?"

"No. No, what's the point?"

"Don't kill it then."

"I have to."

"No you don't."

"Listen, I'll blow it, man, I just know I will."

"Look, Peter, sooner or later you're going to have to say no to your father. And mother. It might as well be now."

"I've got to do it. Just this one time. Then I can say no."

"Okay."

"It's just so fucking banal."

"Just ice up your mind when it's time to shoot. Concentrate, slow yourself down. You'll have more time than you might expect."

"I don't know. . . ."

"It will all be very confused, frantic, noisy—shut everything out except the cat. And slow yourself down."

"Like shooting at a target?"

"No. Like shooting at a fine animal."

"Be there. Just be there."

"I'll be there."

"Are you ever scared of these cats?"

"Sometimes, when I think about what could go wrong."

"I'll blow it. I know I will. I blow everything."

"Maybe that's because you're doing things for other people. Do it for yourself and you'll be all right."

"Will you help me?"

"Of course I will."

"I mean, Jesus, I've got to do this one thing, one time."

"Look," Ben said, "we're going up to look at the cats soon. You'll feel better when you see your jaguar. What is real is always less of a threat than what's imagined."

"Yeah? You know, I think you're wrong about that, Mr. Pearce."

Three

The vehicle route into the foothills was just a winding trail through sage and mesquite and prickly pear cactus, gradually climbing until when it reached the piñon pine country it became the rutted bed of a long-dried creek. A swirling cornucopia-shaped cloud of dust erupted beneath the truck's rear tires. It was still fairly cool, but a certain stinging dryness in the air indicated that it would be hot later in the day.

They sat four abreast in the front seat of the pickup: Ben driving, Mrs. Stuart next to him, then the boy, and then Tom Stuart, next to the open window.

Ben followed the creek bed for another mile and then turned right, eased the truck up over the reddish clay bank, and then ran a kind of slalom course through the widely spaced trees. This was a transitional area between the upper Sonoran desertic and the subalpine zones; piñon and juniper grew here, and scrub oak, and a few tamarisks. To the east the land continued rising, fold upon fold, up into the subalpine zone, then alpine, and finally into the high meadows and ridges and peaks above timberline, a last zone corresponding in flora and climate to the arctic tundra. That was Ben's favorite place: a high, wind-scoured land where marmots stared at you from piles of rock, and if you were lucky you might hear the piercing scream of an eagle.

He stopped the truck in a small clearing and switched off the engine. "We'll have to walk the rest of the way," he said.

"How far?" Meredith Stuart asked.

"About a mile. Take it slow—you folks aren't adjusted to the altitude yet."

"There are a lot of things I'm not adjusted to," she said quietly.

"Is this still your land?" Stuart asked.

"Here it is, yes. Forest Service land starts about two hundred yards east of here. I keep the cats on government land. That way, if anyone stumbles onto them I don't know anything."

Stuart smiled and nodded. "They couldn't guess who owned the cats, though, could they, Ben?"

"Oh, they could guess all right. But guesses alone won't get me into court."

They got out of the truck. There was no wind, no sound. Ben could smell dust and piñon and sage. The sun was fairly high now, and the sky had been bleached of a shade of blue, but it was still dark and glowing, and there were no clouds.

They looked west over the reddish soil of the desert, beyond the plains and the crooked slash of the Rio Grande Gorge, beyond the buttes and mesas, their eyes naturally seeking the horizon, where finally the contours of land were veiled with bluish mist. And forty miles away to the south, the brown, fluted, snow-patched peaks of the Truchas Mountains rose into the humming sky.

Ben waited until they had sated themselves on the view, and then he said, "Why don't you folks lead the way? You'll pick up the path over there. If I lead I'll go too fast and you'll tire yourselves keeping up. Choose your own pace."

Ben wanted to see how well they moved through rough country. They would not be using their fine Mercedes-Benz automobile to track down the cats. It was essential that he learn something about their physical condition, pace, style. He was looking for economy of motion, even grace.

They started off on the path through the brushy trees. Stuart, of course, went first—he was not a man who could tolerate following. He was thirty pounds overweight, and yet he moved lightly, almost delicately, though much too fast considering that he was not accustomed to the altitude. Perhaps he had taken Ben's advice as a challenge. Still, the man moved with the lazy loose-jointed grace of an athlete. And he had done a lot of hunting; he knew how to move through the woods.

Meredith Stuart followed. She too moved well, less relaxed than her husband, more self-aware, but with a kind of tense feline smoothness. She walked with the slightly artificial grace of a dancer.

The boy had a difficult time of it. He could not breathe freely because of his asthma—Ben had expected that—but he was ridiculously clumsy as well. He stumbled over rocks and roots, falling once, and his arm and leg movements were poorly coordinated; his body fought itself, destroying balance and accelerating fatigue. Ben had never seen so awkward a boy. His father moved like an out-of-shape defensive end, his mother like a ballerina; but the boy reminded Ben of a newborn colt, all rubbery legs and dependency and confusion. Christ, Ben thought, I hope the dogs tree that jaguar quickly, because I don't want to run all over these hills with that kid while he's carrying a loaded rifle.

After a few hundred yards of climbing they left the juniper and piñon and entered the ponderosa pine forest. There was a damp, resinous smell here. An inch-thick layer of brown conifer needles covered the ground. Columns of sunlight angled down through the trees and burst into dazzling pools. The path steepened, and Ben could see that the Stuarts were tiring.

"Why don't we stop here and rest for a moment?" he said.

Stuart halted, turned. "I'm all right," he said. "Mere? Peter?" He was breathing deeply and rapidly, his face was red, and the veins in his neck and temples bulged.

"There's no hurry," Ben said.

"How much farther?" Mrs. Stuart asked.

"Not far. Just over the crest of this long hill and then down into the hollow beyond."

There was a rattling sound in the boy's exhalations; he coughed violently for a moment, then sat on a rock.

"Do you need Adrenalin, Peter?" his mother asked.

The boy shook his head.

"There must be a lot of pollen in the air," she said to Ben.

"I don't know. We've had several frosts."

"Ben," Stuart said, "you don't leave those cats up there by themselves, do you?"

"No. Bernard—he's an Indian who works for me off and on—stays up there."

"All the time?"

"He doesn't mind. I relieve him if he wants to go into town for a couple of days. When he get tired of it all he'll go off on a three-week drunk. But until he falls off the wagon he camps up here, feeds and waters the cats and tries to keep them healthy."

The boy lifted his head. "Will he be there now?"

"Yes, you'll meet him."

"Peter loves Indians," Stuart said. "He's mystical about niggers and Indians. I don't think he knows any."

The boy spat between his feet.

"Four cats must eat a hell of a lot," Stuart said.

"Bernard poaches a deer when he can, though he has to go quite a ways to get one. The deer stay away from the cat smell, naturally. And I sometimes buy an old horse for thirty or forty dollars and we butcher it. But yeah, it's quite a job keeping the cats fat and fit. Well, look, shall we go on now? Just this steep stretch to the top and then down the other side."

The camp was located in a depression, almost a ravine; you could not see it until you crested one of the surrounding hills. And you could not smell the cats until you came down off the hill, out of the breeze; it was a strong, bitter stink that seemed to burn the nostrils and throat. Bernard worked hard to keep the area clean; he scrubbed the cage floors with soap and water, buried the feces, burned fires of the perfumed piñon, but still, there were four big cats here, meat eaters, confined in a relatively small area, and it was impossible to completely eliminate the odor. There had been thousands of flies buzzing around during the summer, but the frosts had killed them.

It was not the worst of camps: tall fir trees encircled the clearing; a sweetwater spring trickled out of a jumble of reddish-gold rocks at the south end of the hollow; there was a level site well away from the cages for an eight-by-twelve canvas tent; Bernard had built a large firepit and lined it with rocks and covered it with an iron grill; and he'd even packed up a few hundred pounds of good adobe soil and some straw and made himself a Pueblo-style oven for baking Indian bread.

"Where's Bernard?" the boy asked.

"He probably heard us coming, didn't know who we might be, and ran out into the woods. He'll be back."

"Christ," Stuart said. "Let's have a look at them goddamned cats."

The cats were contained in a fifty-foot-long, eight-foot-wide cage divided into five equal sections. One of the pens was empty now. Each cat had a ten-by-eight-foot space, really not enough for proper exercise, but they could pace and circle and remain in adequate health. The pens had been built of closely spaced aspen saplings covered inside and out with heavy chicken wire. The floors, roofs, and wall partitions were made of half-inch plywood.

The female mountain lion lay at the rear of her pen, sleepily watching them.

Peter glanced at the lioness and then, anxious to see his jaguar, moved down the line of cages.

"She's small," Stuart said.

"About one hundred pounds," Ben said. "That isn't bad for a female."

Stuart silently watched the cat. "Is she sick?"

"No, just lazy. She's used to humans now. She and the male are much calmer than the jaguar and the leopard—especially the leopard. The leopard's been caged and around people ever since he was a cub, but he's still terribly nervous, he's electric."

"How much for her?" Meredith Stuart asked.

"Twenty-five hundred dollars."

"Will you let her go if I buy her?"

"Sure," Ben said. "You can have her for two thousand dollars if you want her released."

"Don't talk horseshit, Mere," Stuart said. "If we buy her, we'll use her. I'll maybe kill her with my bow."

"I have my own money," she said softly.

"Just forget it."

Peter walked toward them. "Mr. Pearce, which one is the jaguar?"

"The one in the last cage."

"Oh. I couldn't tell the difference."

"Jaguars are built thicker, heavier than leopards. They're not nearly as graceful-looking. And jaguars have one or two spots inside the rosette designs on their fur. Leopards don't have markings inside the ro-settes. Go back and look again—you'll see. Hell, you should *feel* which one is the leopard."

The boy left and Ben and the Stuarts moved down a few feet and looked into the second pen. The male mountain lion was dozing at the rear of his cage, sprawled out, whiskers twitching. "Hey!" Ben shouted. The cat lifted his fine, small head, gazed at them, yawned, and then collapsed.

"He'll go about one hundred and forty pounds," Ben said. "A fine animal."

"He acts like a house tabby," Stuart said in disgust.

"He's a little cage-stale," Ben said. "Anyway, Bernard fed the cats this morning. They're full of food and water, docile." That was a lie: Bernard fed the cats three times a week but never the day before a hunt; they should be fast then, alert, in order to give the hunter some excitement for his money. Although hell, there was a woman from California who'd wanted to kill her cat while it was still in the cage. Not that she was frightened; she simply wanted to have killed a big cat, and she didn't see why she should have to sweat for the trophy. Ben had con-trived to make her run up and down hills for half a day—she'd sweated all right.

Stuart looked at his wife. "What do you think, Mere?"

"He's beautiful," Meredith Stuart said.

"Do you like him?"

"I love him." Her whispery voice sounded remote; similar, Ben thought, to the voice of someone who is suffering extreme pain but is unwilling to admit it. Like his father's voice toward the end.

The jaguar was pacing counterclockwise around the cage, padding along in that low, slope-shouldered, rippling way that cats have. It was almost a sloppy walk, but you could see the latent quickness and power. The jaguar, in her noble cat-arrogance, refused to look at them; they did not exist. She paced around the perimeter of the cage as if she were on a journey of a hundred miles.

"Now," Stuart said. "That's a cat."

The jaguar plodded on.

"She's not quite full grown, and she'll still go about one hundred and fifty pounds," Ben said.

"Yes, that one's a cat."

"You think so?" Ben said. "Let's look at the leopard."

Peter was standing close to the leopard's cage. He looked over at them. "God," he said.

"Your jaguar's over here, Peter," Ben said. "That's the leopard."

"I know."

At first glance the leopard was almost a disappointment; he was leaner, rangier, less powerful-looking than the jaguar. But then you gradually became aware of something—intensity? A suppressed rage? Hatred? Whatever, it was an emanation; it burned in the cat's opaque yellow eyes, lifted the fur along his spine, invested his movements with a terrible beauty. This cat was more alive than any other creature Ben had ever seen.

"Look," Ben said. "He's stalking us."

"No," Stuart said.

"Watch."

Ben thought this cat was insane. Insane in the

sense that it had been a prisoner all its life and was therefore aberrant from wild members of the species; and insane too because it seemed to carry catness to an extreme—it was wholly cat, more cat than other cats; it was a kind of logical monster.

"A big leopard," Ben said. "About one hundred and seventy pounds, maybe more. He doesn't look that heavy, but he is. Look at the thickness of bone."

The leopard did not circle the cage as the jaguar had; he paced from wall to wall, close to the screened poles, staring at them as he passed, turning, coming back again, watching them, turning, stalking.

"I didn't get my leopard in Africa," Stuart said quietly.

"Here's your leopard," Ben said.

The leopard's fur shined with a kind of shot-silk yellow (you saw blurs of gold, fawn, orange, and ocher in his coat), and the rosettes were coal-black against the yellow and seemed to vibrate. Ben thought that it was difficult to *see* this cat. You could look at him but never really apprehend him; and if you closed your eyes you might picture a leopard but not this leopard. He was special. Some animals so exceed their biological norm that they acquire an aura of greatness. Ben sometimes had to fight the temptation to regard this leopard as somehow magical. (Bernard, the Indian animist, who saw something magical in everything dead or alive, had suggested the notion.) But the leopard was a cat—a great cat, but still only a cat.

Stuart seemed to sense the greatness, and so did his wife and son. Ben liked them for that; their silent respect and fear went a long way toward making up for their insensitivity in other areas.

And now the cat crouched in the center of the cage, facing them. His head was low, his hindquarters slightly elevated. He sought their eyes.

"I told you," Ben said. "Watch this now."

The cat slowly inched toward them across the floor of the cage. They could see his teeth now, the long, curved, wetly gleaming canines and the sharp-ridged molars behind. His whiskers were drawn back. His breathing had changed. The tip of his tail hooked nervously, not back and forth as with most cats, but up and down. Then he drew his forefeet beneath his body and began moving his hind feet in place, seeking purchase. He was staring intently, madly, at Peter.

The boy involuntarily cried out and backed away. The cat rose to his feet and resumed pacing.

"He was staring at me!" Peter said.

"Jesus Christ," Stuart said. "He was, goddamn it, he was staring right into Peter's eyes."

"Why me?" the boy asked.

"I don't know," Ben said. But he knew: the leopard had instinctively chosen the weakest member of the group.

"My God, Pearce, you were right, that is a cat."

"I told you he was something special."

Stuart was grinning.

"Do you still think I'm asking too much money for him?"

"My God, he's—it's like he's on *fire*."

Ben looked at Meredith Stuart. She was not frightened like her son, nor exultant like her husband; she seemed transfixed by the animal, hypnotized. Her body was rigid, her eyes were wide and unfocused as she stared into the cage—her eyes did not follow the cat as he paced back and forth across her field of vision.

"Mere!" Stuart said, suddenly angry. "Stop that, hear? Right now!"

"What?" she whispered.

"Aw, Meredith, god*damn* it!"

"Let's have some coffee now, okay?" Ben said. He lightly touched her arm; the muscles were raised and rigid, hard to the touch, but then she relaxed and slowly exhaled. She licked her lips, turned, and looked up at Ben. They were standing very close, and he saw that her ultramarine eyes were dilated—the irises had expanded to half the diameter of the pupils. She licked her lips again, smiled at him, and there was something new in her expression that confused him as much as her earlier trancelike state. (Late that night he awakened and realized that the cat, then his touch, had aroused her sexually.)

They all started walking toward the firepit. "I know Bernard's got some coffee around here somewhere," Ben said nervously. "Who would like a cup?"

No one replied. Stuart and his wife and son were isolated in another of their queer, guilty family silences.

The Stuarts sat together on a split cedar log while Ben made some cowboy coffee, dumping a handful of grounds into the pot and filling it with cold spring water. There were still some orange coals glowing beneath the white ash in the firepit, left over from Bernard's breakfast fire, and Ben kicked the grill aside and set the pot directly on the coals. He washed four cups at the spring and returned.

"I wonder where the hell that old scoundrel Bernard is," Ben said, trying to break the mood.

The Stuarts did not look at Ben, or at each other.

"What do you think of the leopard, Tom?" Ben asked.

Stuart cleared his throat. "Some cat," he said.

"Peter, do you like the jaguar?"

The boy nodded and looked down at his hands.

Ben rummaged around in the boxes of supplies and found a can of condensed milk and a box of sugar.

"We'll take the mountain lion tomorrow morning," Ben said. "Mrs. Stuart's cat. If that's all right."

"Fine," Stuart said.

"Mrs. Stuart?"

"Yes," she said.

"After lunch we can tour the area, if you'd like. There are some places that might interest you."

Peter looked up. The asthma crackled in his voice. "Can we visit the Indian village?"

"Sure. That's one of the places I was going to take you."

"Father. Can we?"

"I don't know. Mere?"

"Yes," she said.

"Okay," Stuart said.

The boy seemed alert now. "Is the pueblo interesting?"

"Why, I'd say so, yes."

"Do they mind if white people go there?"

"Well, they earn a little money off visitors. There's a parking fee, camera fee, and some shops."

"Will there be dances or any ceremonies?"

"Today? No."

"Have you ever seen their ceremonies, Mr. Pearce?"

"No. They're a secretive people, and the ceremonies that have real meaning to them are forbidden to outsiders. The idea is that magic loses its power if the rituals are revealed."

"What kind of religion is it?"

"Well, most of them are Catholics, but they've kept their old religion too. To my mind it's like all primitive religions in that it's based on a terror of nature. The magical rites are an attempt to control nature, or at least to avoid arousing nature's hostility."

"But they love nature, don't they?"

"Yeah, but they're scared of it, too. I don't know, but it seems to me that they fear nature more than they love it."

"Does Bernard follow the religion?"

"Off and on. Off and on for sixty years. Bernard doesn't live out at the village, and he can't return until he's gone through certain purification rites. He's impure now, and he's been impure for as long as I've known him. He talks about going back, but he never does. Maybe the council won't let him. But he wears his hair long, in pigtails, and he knocks the heels off his store shoes, and he usually wears a blanket, but he never quite gets around to being purified."

The coffee was boiling now. Ben used his folded handkerchief to remove the pot from the coals. He snatched off the lid, then fetched a cup of cold water from the spring and poured it over the coffee to settle the grounds.

"I don't know where the son of a bitch is now," Ben said.

"Hey, who you calling son a bitch, Ben?" Bernard yelled. He was picking his way down the steep hill behind them. He carried his old single-shot twenty-gauge in one hand and a wild hen turkey in the other.

"Look at that," Ben said. "Out of season and a hen besides."

"You bet."

"Try to tell an Indian about game laws."

"Tell yourself about game law, Ben."

Bernard was in his early seventies; his hair was pure white, parted in the center, and pulled tightly back in two shoulder-length ropes that were wrapped with red cloth. His skin was brown and deeply lined around the mouth and eyes. His teeth were yellow and crooked. He had the typical Pueblo Indian build: he was about five feet five inches, broad and thick through the chest, short-waisted, with short bowed legs. He walked with a toe-in rolling gait. Today he wore a baseball cap, a red plaid shirt, baggy khaki trousers, and a J.C. Penney blanket was tied shirt-like around his middle. Grinning, he reached level ground, dropped the turkey, and propped his shotgun against a tree.

The Stuarts rose from the log.

"Bernard," Ben said, "this is Mrs. Stuart."

He crinkled his eyes and gave her a lingering, limp handshake.

She smiled. "How do you do."

"And Tom Stuart."

He shook Stuart's hand, said, "Hi, brother."

"And Peter."

"Hi, brother. Okay."

"Do you want some coffee, Bernard?"

"Sure, Ben."

The Stuarts sat down on the cedar log. Bernard squatted on his heels. Ben filled the tin cups with coffee and passed them out.

Bernard blew into his coffee. "Benny," he said, "I see some track in the creek mud, you know?"

"Cat?"

"Small one."

"Where?"

"By waterfall, you know."

"Male?"

"Yeah, he scratch. Scratch everywhere." Unlike the younger, better-educated Indians, Bernard spoke English poorly, omitting articles and plurals, confusing tenses; and he spoke with a strong Tewa accent, the words seemingly formed under his tongue and then lazily expelled.

"How old is this track?"

"This morning."

"Christ," Ben said.

"What's this?" Stuart asked.

"Bernard found the tracks of a young male mountain lion."

"Are there many wild lions around here?"

"Damn few on the public lands. We pretty well hunted them out when they were considered varmints, before they were declared game animals. This one was probably chased off Indian land by the older males. I hope his scent doesn't screw up the dogs."

"Yeah," Bernard said.

"Why not go after the wild lion?" Stuart asked.

"He pretty damn small," Bernard said.

Ben said, "We don't want the dogs to run down and tree a young cat and let the big male over there escape."

"Well, that sounds like your problem," Stuart said.

"It is. Finished your coffee? Okay, let's go down and have lunch and then go sightseeing. Bernard, do you want to go into town today?"

"Naw. This pretty good right here, Ben."

"You're a demented bush Indian."

"That right."

"Tomorrow at nine o'clock, Bernard. The male mountain lion."

"Sure," he said.

Ben rose to his feet. "Let's go," he said to the Stuarts.

That afternoon Ben took the Stuart family to the bridge over the six-hundred-foot-deep Rio Grande Gorge ("Any trout down there?" Stuart asked. "Big trout," Ben said.); up the Rio Hondo Canyon road to the ski valley to see the groves of glossy yellow fall aspens; to the shops and galleries in town; to the old Kit Carson house; and finally Ben took them out to the Indian pueblo, where they behaved as if they were visiting an outdoor anthropology museum instead of an actual community. They wandered into the forbidden kiva areas despite the warning signs, entered an old woman's house and looked around, and took photographs of people without first asking permission. Ben was embarrassed; he had friends out here.

The pueblo lay at the base of a twelve-thousand-foot mountain, and the two major housing complexes were divided by a stream fed by the Indians' sacred Blue Lake. The cube-shaped adobe rooms were stacked one atop the other in a sort of aboriginal apartment-house style.

"Do they let white men hunt up in those mountains?" Stuart asked.

"No," Ben said.

The boy was romantically impressed with the Indians and their semi-primitive way of life; he saw the pueblo as a kind of super commune of anti-technology, mystical nature worshippers, which of course it was. He was right. Meredith Stuart was quiet most of the afternoon, remote but not unhappy, and then, in a softly bitter way, nearly whispering, she said that the village was sad sad sad, a sad mud ghetto. And she was right. Stuart saw the Indians as fools, living in poverty while owning more than one hundred thousand acres of prime timber, mineral, grazing, and recreation land. Stuart was right, too.

It seemed to Ben that you could hardly guess wrong about these Tewa Indians; they were what you wanted them to be, like your illusions. Despite their pickup trucks and Winchester rifles and all, they had chosen to remain psychologically a Stone Age people. They had preserved their old ways into a time of moon walks. Most professed to be Catholics, and they were, but they had an older, simpler, more obscure religion as well, one that would be perfectly intelligible to the ancient cave dwellers of Lascaux and Altamira. They were like an ant colony or beehive, Ben thought without contempt; there seemed to be one heart, one brain, a single sourceless will working toward an end that will be exactly the same as the beginning. One will, one need, a relentless, pigheaded march into the centrifuge of time.

Four

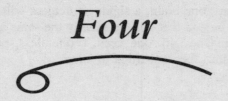

*B*en, hung over, could not eat breakfast, so he left the Stuarts and Mrs. Jaramillo in the kitchen and went outside.

It was another frosty blue morning, exactly like yesterday morning and probably, Ben thought, exactly like tomorrow morning. The ground was frozen hard and dusted with frost. (By eleven o'clock the grounds would be a slimy mud wallow; adobe soil was like concrete when moisture had been frozen in, and like quickmud when thawed.) Ravens cawed and fluttered from branch to branch in the yellow cottonwoods. The iron-spear fence and the crosses in the cemetery slanted crookedly against the turquoise horizon. He could smell piñon-wood smoke, sage, dead leaves, rotting fruit in the orchard. The mountains rose abruptly out of the plain and climbed steeply into the luminous sky. Up high, groves of aspens shined like burnished gold epaulets on the shoulders of the mountains. Rivers and lakes of shadow lay in the low folds of desert to the west.

He heard the house door slam. He turned: Stuart had just come out on the open porch, and he stood there, legs apart, yawning and scratching his sides. He was a tall man, but standing on the elevated platform, in his high-heeled cowboy boots and big hat, he looked eight feet tall.

"Goddamn," he rumbled in his phlegmy voice. "This much fresh air could kill a city dweller."

His belly hung down over his belt, half concealing the tarnished silver steerhead buckle. He was wearing the ebony cowboy boots, tight-fitting whipcord Western trousers, a natural chamois shirt, a faded, fleece-lined Levi's jacket, and the fuzzy pearl-colored Stetson.

Stuart yawned again, closing his eyes and twisting his jaw to the side. "Damn," he said.

"Sleep okay?" Ben asked.

"Just fine." Stuart stepped down off the porch. He still looked big at ground level, but he wasn't a giant now. He had not shaved this morning. There was a dried flake of egg yolk at the corner of his mouth.

"I told Meredith to hurry along," Stuart said.

"There isn't any rush."

"You don't know Mere. She could dawdle to next Tuesday."

"Does Mrs. Stuart have her own rifle?" Ben asked.

"No, she'll be using one of mine."

"What is it?"

"A Savage .270. A real fine, reliable old rifle."

"Well . . ."

"Isn't that enough gun?"

"It should be okay if she's using hollow-point or soft-nosed ammunition. I don't like it if she'll have steel-jacketed bullets."

Stuart grinned. "I gave her dumdums, that's what she's using."

"Fine. What we're looking for is a lot of shocking power—something that will stun the cat, tear him up, break bone, even if the shot isn't where it should be."

"I'll take along my 30.06," Stuart said.

"No, don't bring a gun."

Stuart cocked his head.

"I'll back her up with my shotgun."

"Another rifle won't hurt."

"Look, Mr. Stuart, I have—"

"Now goddamn, Ben, every time you've had bad news you call me 'Mr. Stuart.' What is it this time?"

"I have a rule that there can only be two guns in any party, mine and the hunter's."

"Ben, come *on,* now."

"I took a big party out last summer and they were all armed. The cat jumped down out of the tree and everyone got excited and started shooting. There were bullets whizzing every which way. One of the dogs got shot. Bernard got a bullet hole through his blanket—he stays the hell away now until the shooting is over."

"Where were those people from?"

"Los Angeles."

"Well, what do you expect from *them*, Ben?"

"You and Peter are welcome to come along, of course, but—"

"We thank you," Stuart said dryly.

"—but I'd like to keep you well back so you don't distract the cat. Or Mrs. Stuart. Or me."

Stuart stared levelly at Ben for a time, and then he very softly said, "Ben, I don't understand it, but you seem duty-bound to frustrate my every desire."

"I'm sorry. But I've got to control these hunts. They're my responsibility."

"Ben, I'm paying good money, a lot of money."

"I know, but you'll pay a doctor or lawyer good money and not tell him how to do his job. Think of it that way."

"Ben, hear now, I think I'm at *least* as good a hunter as you are. I've shot in Africa, Alaska, British Columbia, Yucatan—don't you trust me with a gun?"

"We've got to do this my way."

Stuart turned and looked out over the desert. "Ben, I don't believe you're dumb. Are you dumb? You're in trouble here. They're eating you alive, and in about six months they're going to be cracking your bones for marrow. I'm a rich man. I like you, Ben. Now why do you want to keep going head-up against a rich man who could help you? I *like* to help people, Ben, and that's the truth. I've helped a lot of men."

"I haven't asked for any help."

"I know that. But you've thought about asking, haven't you?"

"Do you only help men who kiss your ass?"

Stuart slowly turned and looked at him. "Hell, yes, Ben! Of course!"

"I'll go get the dogs," Ben said.

"Don't you kiss ass, Ben? Not even a little?"

"I haven't yet. But I've kicked ass a few times."

Stuart grinned.

The kennels were kept on the far side of the old adobe shed. The dogs somehow seemed to sense when there was going to be a hunt; they howled and barked much of the night, and when he came for them in the morning they whined and cowered and lost control of their bladders and hurled themselves against the chicken-wire fence. They loved to hunt, were pee-eager, and Ben thought they were probably also the worst lion pack in the Southwest. The old blue tick and bloodhound cross was pretty good, and so was the Airedale, but the other six were untrained curs that Ben had "adopted" from the town animal shelter. They were just about useless on the trail. The only good thing Ben could say about them was that they generally followed the leadership of the hound and Airedale, and contributed enough noise and confusion to intimidate a cat.

Ben opened the gate, and the dogs rushed through, almost knocking him down. They were shivering with excitement, moving in circles, yawning, wetting, sniffing the ground and air.

He walked around the corner of the shed, and the dogs followed. Stuart had not moved; he was still standing at the base of the porch steps, breathing steam, hands in back pockets, back slightly arched, potbelly hanging down over his belt. He watched Ben approach and then swiveled his head and looked at the dogs one by one.

"That's the sorriest-looking pack I've ever seen," he said.

"The hound and the Airedale are good," Ben said.

"They all look like shit eaters to me."

"They'll tree a cat, and that's all we need."

"Ben, I surely hope you know what you're about."

The door opened and Mrs. Stuart came out onto the porch.

Ben removed his hat and then, feeling foolish, jammed it back on his head. "Good morning," he said.

She wore no makeup, and the dark blue of her eyes was startling against the pallor of her skin. Her lips were wet and bruised-looking. She gazed gravely at Ben for a moment, and then she smiled.

"Where's the rifle, Mere?" Stuart said.

"Peter is bringing it for me," she said.

"Christ, honey, you can carry your own rifle, can't you?"

She looked out over the pastel desert. "My, this early-morning air is like fire."

Today she wore a waist-length wolfskin jacket and a matching wolfskin Cossack-style hat. Her blond hair escaped the hat and flowed down over her shoulders. She wore jeans, and over the jeans flared leather chaps with silver conchos, hammered out of old silver pesos, down the outside seams, and a pair of brown cowboy boots.

Costumes, Ben thought in disgust. It seemed that no one wore clothes anymore, they dressed in costumes. On any summer day on the town plaza you could see buffalo hunters, white hunters, mountain men, yachtsmen, Oriental holy men, cowboys, gunfighters, guerrilla fighters, homesteaders, Peruvian peasants, Greek fishermen, Caucasian Indians, and Africans. . . . Nearly everyone was wearing costumes; the only difference was that the rich could change costumes and identities several times a day, while all the others were trapped in their roles for weeks and months at a time.

Ben crossed the yard and started the pickup truck's engine. He got out, scraped the frost off the windows, then whistled up the dogs and got them to climb into the camper shell.

He returned to the cab and pushed a radio button. An evangelist with an almost incomprehensible West Texas accent was attacking socialists and other free-loading parasitic mongrel scum: "Aw Mighty Gawd heps em what heps emseves." He pushed another button and heard that kind of jumpy accordion-dominated Mexican music that reminded him of pol-kas.

The Stuarts, across the yard by the porch, were talking; or rather, Tom Stuart talked while his wife listened. She appeared angry—no, not angry, sullenly proud. Her chin was high, and her eyes were half-lidded.

Ben tried another radio station: someone was say-ing that New Mexico ranked forty-seventh in the na-tion in per capita income. "Yeah," Ben said. He pushed another button: weather news, an early snow-storm in Montana, heavy rains in the Gulf states . . .

Stuart was still talking to his wife. Scolding her again, Ben thought. It didn't matter why. Tom Stuart rarely addressed his wife unless it was to scold her for something she had done, criticize her for some-thing she was doing, or shame her for something she might do in the future. He was usually gentle with her, almost sadly sweet at moments, and she seemed to have acquired a near immunity to his criticism; but still, it was a brutal process.

And now Peter came out onto the porch. Pale, thin, somber. At least the boy was not wearing a costume; or rather, he wore an anti-costume costume: threadbare Levi's with brightly colored patches sewn here and there, a faded denim work shirt, and dirty white sneakers. He was carrying the rifle by the barrel. His father took it away from him, checked the safety, and then demonstrated the correct way to carry a weapon.

Ben turned off the radio. The Stuart family was a unit again, intact and functioning normally.

"Aw Maghty Gawd," Ben said, "hep me."

Ben drove the same route as he had yesterday, through the reddish soil of the sage and chamisa country, climbing all the while, and then along the rutted bed of the dried creek. He drove a hundred yards beyond yesterday's turnoff point, then pulled out and parked among the piñons. The air, a little warmer now, smelled of sun and dust and pine. A few scattered sage bushes, on the fringe of their growth zone, shined a frosty silver in the sunlight.

"We're a little early," Ben said. "I told Bernard to release the cat at nine o'clock. It'll still be fairly cool then, in case we have to do a lot of hiking up and down these hills."

"Don't you have any saddle horses, Ben?"

"Just one."

"Too bad. It might be more fun to hunt those cats from the saddle."

"The country here is no good for that. Too many trees, too much brush."

Stuart slowly nodded. He turned to his wife. "Are you ready, Mere?"

"Yes, she said softly. She was staring straight ahead through the windshield. She seemed calm, almost sleepy.

"Just do as I told you," Stuart said. "Release the safety, aim carefully, squeeze the trigger, don't snatch at it. Hell, you can shoot. I know you can shoot. I've seen you bust the clay birds."

Peter, who had been pale and quiet throughout the drive, now suddenly said, "I think I'm going to throw up," and he opened the door and walked off into the trees.

It was quiet in the truck for a time, and then Meredith Stuart said, "Peter has an upset stomach from the unfamiliar foods." She continued to stare through the windshield.

"Unfamiliar foods my ass," Stuart said.

The woman slid down the seat and stepped outside.

Ben lit a cigarette.

"The boy is going to be all right," Stuart said.

Ben nodded and exhaled smoke.

"Women have babied him too much. His mother, grandmother, teachers . . . Like so many of the goddamned kids today, Peter wants to take the soft and easy way. There ain't any soft and easy way. You know that, Ben. The world is a big rock. You can stand on top of it, or you can lay down underneath and get broken."

Ben made a noise deep in his throat and inhaled cigarette smoke.

"Peter will be okay. I'll make him okay."

"There are different kinds of people," Ben said, exhaling smoke.

"That's right, Ben. There are two kinds—men and women. And Peter, by God, is going to be a man."

"Okay," Ben said.

"He's going to shoot that jaguar. That'll straighten his shoulders a bit. And when we get back home I'm taking him to the fanciest whorehouse in Dallas-Fort Worth. It's pathetic, him being a virgin at his age, in these times. He has some learning to do, that boy, but he's going to be all right."

"We have about ten more minutes," Ben said. "Let's get a little sun."

He opened the door, slid out, and walked around to the other side of the truck. Meredith Stuart was standing about twenty yards away, looking down over the dry folds of desert to the shadowed, lightninglike slash of the gorge. Her legs were slightly spread; her hands were at her sides. She had removed the wolf-skin hat and her sun-sheened hair was free to flow in the faint breeze. Ben thought that she was posing. Not for him or her husband or son, but more likely for herself: seeing herself from the outside, standing motionless in a certain desolate terrain and evoking a certain mood . . .

Peter walked out of the trees with a cupped hand full of small wild plums. "Are these okay to eat, Mr. Pearce?" he asked.

"Sure, Peter. The frosts might have damaged them, though."

The boy bit into one of the plums, chewed slowly and thoughtfully, then swallowed. "First it's sweet," he said. "And then it tastes kind of dry, but not very bitter. They're good." He turned and started away. "Mother, would you like a wild plum?"

"No thank you, dear," Mrs Stuart called.

Stuart got out of the truck. He was carrying the .270 rifle. "Ben, now what's the drill on these hunts?"

"Bernard will release the cat at nine sharp."

"How does he do that without taking a chance on the cat climbing him like he was a tree?"

"He rigs a pulley system and raises the cat's cage door from inside an empty cage."

"Indian locks himself up, huh?" Stuart said, smiling faintly. "Okay, what happens if the cat decides he likes the cage, or he wants to hang around the area for the free food and the company of the other cats?"

"That hasn't happened yet. I don't think it will. If it does, Bernard will think of something."

"What happens if the dogs catch the airborne scent from the pens and run up there to bark at the caged cats, while the loose one runs ten miles?"

"The wind around here is almost always from the west or southwest. Like today, there isn't much of a breeze, but it's blowing past the dogs toward the cats. Now, I parked north of the pens. The cats always start out north, go that way for a while, and then turn east, toward the high country. Bernard says they go north first to run across the wind, smell what's below them, and then turn east when they hear the spirit of the sacred mountain singing to them. But Bernard believes that Tokay wine caused his arthritis. I don't know why the cats go north and then east—maybe because they somehow sense that that's the quickest way to the wild, high country. I don't know."

"What then?"

"Bernard follows the cat for a distance, and when he gets well away from the cages he blows his dog whistle. We won't hear it, but the dogs will go half crazy when they do."

Stuart nodded. "The Indian will keep blowing the whistle until the dogs reach him."

"Right."

"And the Indian will prevent the dogs from back-tracking down to the pens."

"Yes."

"It sounds hit-or-miss, Ben."

"It's worked okay so far."

"Your show, Ben, but what happens if the cat goes south?"

"Same procedure. Bernard will track him and blow the whistle when he thinks it's time. The dogs will run toward the whistle."

"I'm paying for cats, Ben. Remember that."

"No cat, no dough."

"It's almost nine."

"I'll open the camper window so the dogs can hear the whistle. Why don't you give the rifle to Mrs. Stuart now and maybe calm her down a little?"

"If she was any calmer," Stuart said, "I'd go over there and give her closed heart massage."

Ben walked around to the rear of the truck and cranked open the louvered windows. One of the dogs had shit inside the camper; Ben could smell it.

Meredith and Peter approached. She was wearing her hat again. Her eyes were very cool and direct, issuing challenges.

"Care for a plum, Mr. Pearce?" Peter asked.

"No thank you."

"You were sick a minute ago, boy," Stuart said. "Now you're eating plums."

The boy turned away.

Stuart handed his wife the rifle. "There's a cartridge in the chamber, Mere. The safety is on."

They waited for about ten minutes, and then the dogs began whining and moving around inside the camper; they could hear toenails scratching against the pickup bed.

"Let them out now, Ben?" Stuart said.

"In a few minutes."

Meredith had closed her eyes and turned her face toward the sunlight.

Peter was standing close to his mother. His hands were stuffed in the back pockets of his Levi's.

"The dogs want to go, Ben."

Ben nodded.

"Damn," Stuart said, grinning. "There's nothing like the hunt. My old heart's beating like hell, and I'm not even shooting today. Mere, do you feel it?"

"Mmmm," she murmured.

"Ben, do you know anything that gives you a feeling like the hunt?"

Ben straightened. "Oh, goddamn it," he said. "Look at that."

And then they all saw the cat. The mountain lion came running out of the trees fifty feet away. He was a tawny flash, a blur not much lighter in color than the soil. The cat broke into a patch of open ground, running in long bounds, coiling small and then stretching out, coiling. And then he saw the people and skidded in the dust, spinning around and falling, but he twisted and arose before momentum had ceased and returned toward the mountains.

"Well Jesus Christ," Stuart said.

"Wow!" Peter yelled.

Meredith Stuart was smiling faintly.

"He didn't read your program, Ben," Stuart said.

The cat was gone.

Five

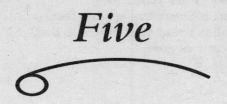

*B*en ran around to the truck cab, got his double-barreled shotgun, returned, and snatched open the camper door. The dogs tumbled out and began to confusedly mill about, sniffing and snapping at the air, trembling and wetting.

"Now remember, Mere," Stuart was saying, "keep the safety on until it's time to shoot."

She nodded, smiling at him. She looked . . . what? Puzzled and ironic.

"Listen to Ben. He'll help you."

She turned away from her husband and looked up toward the mountains.

"Make your shot count, because Ben's twelve-guage'll tear up the pelt."

"This is making me sick," Peter said.

"Let's go," Ben said to her, and he trotted toward

where the cat had fallen. There was a roughened slide mark on the ground and two widely spaced sets of tracks, one leading down from the high country and the other returning. The dogs went a little crazy when they ran into the airborne scent (odor must be like an invisible, spreading cloud, Ben thought); one dog quickly voided its bowels, another began shaking all over in a kind of paroxysm, two more started fighting, and Ben had to step forward and kick them until they separated.

The hound lifted her head and howled, a clear brass horn note, and then she lowered her muzzle to the ground and loped off toward the woods. The Airedale, upper lip peeled to reveal his canine teeth, followed the hound. And then the others, barking and yelping, fell into some kind of status-ordered pack and joined the hunt.

"They won't hurt the mountain lion, will they?" Meredith asked.

"Not likely," Ben said. "It could be the other way around. Come on. If you get tired let me know. And watch where the muzzle of that rifle is aimed."

Ben jogged easily through the juniper and piñon for two hundred yards, and then the land rather abruptly steepened and changed. There were ponderosa pine and blue spruce now, and a few scrub oaks; and the air carried new scents: rot and resin, damp soil, wildness. They moved in and out of the cool shadows. Ben did not slow his pace when the terrain steepened. He glanced over his shoulder from time to time; the woman would fall a little behind and then hurry to close the space between them, fall behind again. Her face was shiny with perspiration, and he could hear the hiss of her exhalations. Tom Stuart and the boy had fallen well back; they were just flashes of color among the trees below.

The country continued to change as they climbed: the trees were taller, more closely spaced, and very little sunlight was able to penetrate the tiered layers of boughs to the forest floor.

The dogs were far above them and a little to the north. Ben listened to their distant barks and the clear brassy song of the hound. The dogs would let him know when the lion had been treed; he would be able to hear the fear and excitement in their voices. He hoped Bernard had done his job. If the dogs back-tracked down to the pens, this hunt was over; the cat would be five miles away before they'd be able to drag the dogs away from the caged animals and back on the trail. This cat was running all over the damned place, down to the desert, back up again, crossing his own tracks—it was going to take a little luck. The dogs would arrive at a point or several points where the trail divided, and it was about fifty-fifty that the hound would follow the wrong scent. Three thousand dollars, Ben thought. Three thousand dollars loose and running.

Ben's eyes burned with sweat, and he could taste salt on his lips. No matter how rapidly and deeply he breathed, he could not get quite enough air; his limbs were being deadened by oxygen deficiency. He knew that there really was no need to push this hard. If the dogs kept to the right trail they would tree the cat. But an obscure rage kept Ben going at the same pace;

rage and the necessity to reach and kill that three thousand dollars. Maybe the rage was a product of the necessity.

And, as on other hunts, he noticed that fatigue seemed to sharpen his perceptions. It was like those Saturday afternoons a long time ago when, in the fourth quarter of a tough football game, he would suddenly become acutely aware of the clean smell of grass, the purity of its greenness, and the fragile saberlike conformation of each individual blade. At such instants he wondered how it was possible not to be aware of the unique color and scent and *integrity* of grass at all times. And he had felt the physical numbness that would in a few hours turn into pain.

It was like that now: he saw in sharp outline the millions of individual brown pine and fir needles that formed a thick mat on the forest floor; the scattered fat pine cones which looked like hand grenades; the veins of an oak leaf that recapitulated in miniature the trunk and branches of its parent tree. Everything was sharply focused, super real, and yet somehow as remote as if perceived in a dream.

Ben finally stopped to rest on the crest of a hill. There was a cooling breeze there, and a good view of the surrounding country. The dogs had moved a little farther to the north.

Meredith Stuart slowly climbed to the top of the hill and, without speaking, handed Ben her rifle and then collapsed supine on the ground. She covered her eyes with her left forearm. One knee was raised. Her lips were moist, parted to show a wet gleam of teeth, and her chest rose and fell in a rapid, nearly desperate rhythm. A bluish-green vein pulsed in her neck.

"Sorry," Ben said. "I ran you too hard, I guess. There was no need for it. You should have told me to stop."

She licked her lips, started to reply, and then just shook her head.

A very tough lady, Ben thought. The face of an angel and the heart of a scorpion.

He glanced at his watch and was surprised to see that only twenty-five minutes had passed since they had seen the mountain lion down on the desert. It seemed much longer than that. They had covered a lot of ground, gained a lot of altitude. He turned and looked back the way they had come; he could not see Tom Stuart and the boy, but he could hear them crashing around in the brush somewhere far below.

"This may not turn out," Ben said. "Cats are fast and strong, but they don't have much stamina. I don't know. The dogs should have treed him by now."

She lowered her arm and looked up at him. Her face was flushed. Ben thought that he had never seen eyes so dark a blue. They were almost purple now, in this light. And steady—she never blinked, her eyes never wavered when she looked at you. She stared at you and she seemed to listen, but you always had the feeling that she was thinking about something else, something you'd prefer not to know.

"The cat really isn't in good shape, either. He's

been caged for months. A wild cat—well, that would be different."

She stared at him.

"We'll see," he said. "The dogs are still running. They think they've got a hot trail. We'll rest here for a bit and see what happens."

She lifted her other knee. She was breathing easier now.

"Where is your wolfskin jacket? And the hat?"

"I threw them away. They were too hot."

"I doubt if we'll be able to find them."

"I don't care."

"They must have been expensive."

"They were. Very."

"Maybe Tom or Peter will see them and pick them up."

She closed her eyes. "I'm thirsty."

"I should have brought a bottle of water. Sorry. There are creeks up here, but none close-by."

He could still hear the dogs. They had moved back toward the south. He looked at his watch: almost a half-hour now.

Stuart, moving very slowly, had appeared among the trees below them. Peter was not yet in view.

"Well, Christ," Ben said, "we might as well go on."

She sat up. "Ticks," she said.

"What?"

"Ticks, wood ticks. They bury their heads under your skin. Rocky Mountain spotted fever."

"Oh. You don't have to worry about that at this time of year."

She stiffly got to her feet and took the rifle from Ben. Then she turned and looked down the hill toward her husband. "Honey," she called.

Stuart stopped and waved.

There were brown fir needles tangled in her hair. Her lips were swollen and dry. She smiled and waved her hand, calling, "Isn't this fantastic fun, darling? Agony!" Then she turned and looked at Ben. "Tom has high blood pressure. He has to take medication. I hope he doesn't have a stroke."

Then Ben heard fear and triumph in the barking of the dogs, and the hound's baying suddenly sounded like the hoarse braying of a donkey.

He grinned at her. "They've got him," he said. "The cat's treed now or soon will be." He broke open his shotgun, checked the shells, and snapped the action closed. The cartridge in the right chamber, the first to fire, contained slugs; the one in the left chamber, number four bird shot. "Let's go," he said.

They followed a curving saddle between two hills, descended into a shallow ravine, and then climbed a long, thickly wooded slope to a ridge. One of the dogs broke away from the pack to greet them. The mountain lion was lying on a low branch of a pine tree. Fur bristled along his spine. His ears were flattened back. He hissed down at the barking and leaping dogs.

"He's beautiful," she whispered.

"A little closer," Ben said. "He won't come down, we can move in. A little further. Okay."

Saliva frothed around the cat's mouth.

"Okay," Ben said.

"Now?" she asked. "Like this?"

"Shoot."

"Can't we let him run some more?"

"Shoot," Ben said. "Now."

"In the head?"

"No, that's a hard shot and you'll damage the skin. Shoot him behind the shoulder and down a little, where the heart and lungs are."

The mountain lion, exhausted, turned his small head and stared steadily at them.

"For Christ's sake, shoot now," Ben said.

Meredith Stuart released the safety, aimed briefly, squeezed the trigger and shot the cat through the heart. It clawed feebly at the branch, eyes dimming, rolled and turned a half revolution before hitting the ground. Ben rushed forward and kicked the dogs away before they could tear the pelt.

Meredith moved next to him and stood quietly, looking down at the cat.

"Good shot," Ben said.

She smiled faintly. "What is this about?"

"What do you feel?"

"I'll have to wait," she said. "I don't feel anything right now."

"It was a hell of a shot."

"How could I miss? He was so close and so still. I didn't know I would be so close to him."

"Lots of people could miss," Ben said. "People get excited. They miss."

"I wasn't excited," she said.

"I know."

She touched the cat with the toe of her boot. "He looks different now."

"He *is* different now."

"A lovely animal. Shall we close his eyes?"

Ben looked at her. "I don't think that's necessary."

Two of the dogs, tails between their legs, glancing sideways at Ben, crept forward and sniffed the dead cat.

"Look," she said. "He moved."

"No, he's dead. He didn't move."

"Really? It seemed to me . . ."

"No. Your shot turned off the world for him."

Tom Stuart slowly emerged from the trees and joined them. His face was dark red and puffy-looking. He inhaled through his mouth, chest expanding, then noisily exhaled through his nostrils.

"Look, Tom," Meredith said, "look how small his ears are, and see the color of his eyes."

Stuart placed his hands on his hips. Shook his head. Inhaled very deeply, held the breath for a moment, and then slowly exhaled. "Good shooting," he said.

"He's beautiful, isn't he?" she asked. "Isn't he beautiful, Tom?" As though she were not certain that the cat really was beautiful; the he could not be beautiful until her husband said so.

Stuart shook his head again. "Perfect shot," he said. "It couldn't have been better placed."

Ben said, "The cat was dead before he hit ground."

"Is that right?"

"The bullet probably severed the aorta."

"Some shot, honey."

"Where is Peter?" Ben asked.

"Coming."

"Did I do right, Tom?" Meredith asked, anxiously looking up at her husband.

Stuart placed his arm around her waist. "Just fine," he said.

Peter, his breath rattling, walked up and stood next to his mother.

"Look at that, boy," Stuart said. "Your mother busted him right in the heart. Clipped the aorta, Ben says." He sounded angry.

Peter silently stared down at the mountain lion, and then he turned and looked at Meredith. "Are you proud, Mother?" he asked softly.

She seemed confused.

"Mother? Are you proud?"

"Look," Ben said, "why don't you three return to the truck. Just keep moving downhill and you'll end up on the desert. You'll see the truck then. I'll stay and keep the dogs away from the mountain lion. Bernard will be here soon and we'll skin it out."

"We'll stay and watch," Stuart said.

"No, Tom, please," Meredith said. "I'm tired. I want to go down now."

"I would be *proud* to stay and watch," Peter said bitterly.

They turned and started walking back down toward the desert.

Ben smoked two cigarettes and then Bernard, carrying his old shotgun in one hand and his skinning knife in the other, walked out of the trees.

"No dog hurt, Ben?"

"No."

Bernard, pigeon-toed and bowlegged, approached the dead cat. "Good shot," he said.

"The woman's crazy, I think."

"Good shot. Do they want meat, Benny?"

"No. You keep it. Wait—give me a quarter. I'll serve it to the sons of bitches for dinner tonight."

Six

*T*he flickering gray light from the television was freezing Meredith's eyes. It had already frozen her teeth and gums (exactly like those times when she had received an injection of novocaine from the dentist), had numbed her fingertips, and now her eyes were becoming cold and hard. She could hear them crackling faintly as they froze. The television was just rapidly shifting patterns of light and shadow now, a drab kaleidoscope. Her eyes had frozen too swiftly to permit her to make a useful adjustment, and now she didn't know if she was focusing on the middle distance, between herself and the TV, or looking far beyond it, through the television and walls to the desert beyond. Peter, lying on the floor, laughed and twisted around to look at her. She did not know if she succeeded in smiling with her numbed lips.

Turn away from the light now.

I can't.

Try.

I can't!

Of course you can. Just turn your head.

My spinal column is frozen now, too.

Nonsense. Turn away. Tom will notice and he'll get angry.

He won't notice. They're drunk and talking about killing animals—this animal, that animal. I I I Me Me Me. Each trying to be sweatier and bloodier and meaner than the other.

The cat today. Oh, he was so beautiful and so sad, that cat. Like fire, like the lightning had been gathered and lovingly molded into flesh and fur and eyes and teeth. He hissed with a sound like static electricity. There were sparks in his fur, yes. Flames leaped up behind his yellow eyes. He recognized me. Oh, yes, he knew me. I knew him, too.

Crazy bitch.

But I don't want to think about the cat right now, I must save him for later. Thinking about him makes me feel very warm and weak, as though I were melting. Yes, it's like those times after a long, very hot bath, and when I get out of the tub I can hardly stand up, I'm so weak. Warm, melted, and clothing feels so breathy light against my skin. I can feel myself thawing a little just thinking about the cat. But I won't think anymore about my cat until I am sure that I'll be alone for hours and can fall down inside myself all the way. Oh, the falling is so beautiful, just slowly spiraling downward in the same way that Alice fell down the rabbit hole. It's dark and you're warm and falling as in a dream, but there isn't any fear.

Oh, the cat bled into me. When he died he looked at me and the fire behind his eyes entered my eyes, and his blood flowed out of him and into my veins. We ate part of him tonight. I ate more than the others. Peter wouldn't take a bite. Tom ate some but he didn't like it. But it was good, a little like pork but with a *wildness*, firm like pork, with a translucent shield of inner skin, but *wild*. That Ben man knew what was fitting, what was right—it would not have been completed if I hadn't eaten the cat.

"Mere?" Tom Stuart said.

She heard the dry crepitation of ice cracking as she turned her head. She tried to smile, and felt her numb, swollen lips curve up on one side and down on the other. "Yes, Tom?" She saw her breath smoke. The men were sitting side by side on the sofa, alcohol and tobacco, sweat and blood, iron and stone, voices that sounded like the creaking of doors.

"Are you all right, Mere?"

"I don't feel well, Tom." Her voice was coming from the television; would they notice? "Would you help me to the room?"

Seven

The Stuart family would not hunt game on Sunday, but Tom Stuart figured that God would not disapprove of some sporty trout fishing on His day. Meredith consented, saying that she would enjoy a picnic and sunbathing on a river beach while the men fished.

"I'll have Anita pack a nice lunch," Ben said.

"Do you want to fish with Ben and me, Peter?" Tom Stuart asked.

"No. Fishing is a bore."

"Sunbathe then," Stuart said contemptuously.

After breakfast the family dressed up in their Cardin and Dior Sunday-go-to-meetin' clothes, climbed into their car, and drove off to the Baptist church in town.

Ben sat quietly on the sofa for a few minutes, then

threw an armful of Sunday papers on the floor and screamed. It felt good. He inhaled deeply, screamed again, threw the rest of the newspapers around, and got up and walked into the kitchen. Mrs. Jaramillo, her hair burnt and frizzy from a bad permanent (she went to the beauty parlor once a month for a bad permanent), her eyes half-closed from the smoke rising from a cigarette stuck in the corner of her mouth, was washing the breakfast dishes and laughing.

"You scream good, Benny," she said.

"Christ."

"Those Tejanos getting you down?"

"They eat my liver every day and it grows back during the night."

"It's the booze eating your liver, Benny. The Tejanos are eating your brain."

Ben began opening and closing cupboard doors.

"What are you looking for?"

"Those quart mason jars."

"What do you want them for?"

"I'm going to make myself a Texas-sized Bloody Mary."

"Make two. The jars are there, under the sink."

Ben got the jars and filled them with ice. "I'm a mad libationist," he said.

"You're a mad something."

"It runs in the family."

"I know. Your father was crazy too."

"I know, but he was the kind of crazy who didn't have fun."

"How much fun do you have, Benny?"

"Don't ask. Was my grandfather crazy too?"

"Sure he was."

"How do you know? You were just a little girl when he died."

"I heard stories."

"What kind of stories?"

"He was a Penitente for a couple of years. An Anglo Penitente, Benny."

"That's mad, but it's heroic, too."

"His back was all scarred from whippings and wearing cactus."

Ben laughed.

"He wanted to be Christ, but they wouldn't let him. He hadn't been a member long enough."

"Everyone should be Christ at least once."

"He wanted to be symbolically crucified, you know, at the Morada."

"With actual nails, no doubt. How else was my grandfather crazy?"

"He killed a horse that threw him. An expensive horse."

"To hear the legends of those days, everyone killed a horse that threw him."

"No," Mrs. Jaramillo said. "It's true."

"Those were better days, 'Nita. There's no glory in killing your pickup truck."

"Once, when I was little, he made my aunt—your grandfather's second wife, Benny—he made her dance here in this house until she dropped from exhaustion."

"Why?"

"She liked to dance. She was young and she liked to dance. Your grandfather hated dancing and he hated to see her dancing with the young men. So he made her dance all night once after a regular dance. You know? She never danced after that."

Ben shook his head. "Was my grandmother crazy?"

"No."

"My mother? I don't remember much about her."

"No, they both died young."

"That sounds like a profound non sequitur. Do you want horseradish in your Bloody Mary?"

"Sure, everything."

"Well, I'm not colorful crazy like my male ancestors. I'm dull crazy. Worcestershire?"

"Everything. You're colorful enough, Benny. Too colorful some of the time. That's why your wives walked out."

"Bitches."

"The second one was a bitch, the first one was nice. I liked her."

Ben finished making the quart Bloody Marys—ice, vodka, tomato juice, lime, Tabasco sauce, Worcestershire sauce, salt and pepper, celery stalks, and a bit of mashed onion.

"*Salud,*" Ben said.

"*Salud.*" Mrs. Jaramillo tasted her drink, licked the red off her upper lip, and smiled. "Very good," she said.

"*Que viva la fiesta,*" Ben said.

"*Que viva la fiesta,* Benny."

They clinked their glasses together and drank again.

"Did they enjoy the cat?" Mrs. Jaramillo asked.

"She did. Stuart and the kid looked sick at dinner."

"That was cruel of you, Benny."

"Well, as my deranged father used to tell me: 'Son, if you kill something you got to eat it.' He once made me eat a magpie I'd shot. A magpie! It didn't taste like chicken, 'Nita."

"Chicken doesn't taste like chicken anymore."

"Yeah, well, it doesn't yet taste like magpie."

"It will soon."

" 'Nita, it's Sunday. Have you got anything scheduled for this afternoon?"

"Well, there's a Rosary for the Mondragon boy."

"Which Mondragon is that?"

"Chucho's son. He was killed in the car accident."

"Oh, yeah. Another teenage kamikaze. Okay, 'Nita, why don't you pack a lunch for us Texans and then take off."

"Do you want me to come back and cook dinner?"

"No, I'll fry fish if we catch some, or barbecue some steaks."

"I'll stay with my sister tonight then."

"Fine."

She touched his hand. "Benny, keep trying to have a good time, but don't be crazy."

"Sure."

"I mean it."

"Vamos a ver," he said.

"Yes, we'll see."

The Stuarts returned from church at eleven thirty, changed clothes and gathered their gear, and then got into Ben's pickup for the drive to the river. Ben stopped at a general store in Ranchos, where Stuart bought a three-day fishing license and some flies which were often successful in the local streams. Ben drove south again for a few miles and then turned west on a dirt road that led across the flat desertic plain: sage, cactus, tumbleweed, stony reddish soil, a dry herbal heat. There was a fine view of the snow-powdered Sangre de Cristo Mountains to their right, and the long-distance-blued stretch of desert and butte country straight ahead. It was another transparent, sparkling day; everything, land and sky and shadow, seemed to be made of colored glass. Ben had the feeling he should be able to look through the mountains to the mountains beyond; or even, if he wished, get out of the truck and kick a boulder into a thousand glittering shards. These pellucid autumn days always seemed to promise an adventure, a chance to transcend the past and his limitations. He expected something wonderful or terrible to occur which would make him different, better, happy. Nothing ever happened, but that did not prevent him from faithfully believing that on *this* crystal day . . .

The road curved to the south, and a deep, steep-walled canyon appeared on their right. Time to play tour guide again.

"That's the Taos Creek Gorge," Ben said. "It converges with the Rio Grande Gorge down below. Look over the side, you'll see the wreckage of some cars. Every now and then, a drunk misses a curve or drifts over the side."

"Don't tell us about it until we're down," Meredith said. She closed her eyes.

The narrow, rocky road had been carved out of one of the canyon walls. They could look across empty space to the other wall, or down to the creek. The road descended in a nearly straight line, then there were some loopy switchbacks, and then the terrain opened up and they could see the sun-silvered river. Ben eased the truck around the last switchback; there was a short, furious rapids to their right, and downstream a steel bridge, broad sandy banks, and a sand island around which the river divided into two shallow channels.

"The river looks low," Stuart said.

"It is. Low, slow, and clear at this time of year. A good time to take trout."

Ben drove for another quarter mile, passed the bridge, then turned off and parked by the water. He switched off the ignition. They sat quietly for a moment, listening to the sounds of the river: soft splashing, a hum from the rapids above, and a deeper, fainter vibration that was as much sensed as heard. The only other sound was the ratchety buzzing of some cicadas. It was bright and very hot.

They unloaded everything from the truck: a blanket, wicker picnic basket, a Styrofoam cooler filled with beer and Coke, the fishing equipment.

"Are we going to fish right here, Ben?" Stuart asked.

"No, we'll hike partway up the gorge. There's some fine trout water back there."

"What kind of trout?"

"Brown, rainbow, cutthroat."

Peter had picked up a handful of pebbles and was throwing them out into the river. He threw awkwardly, frozen at the wrist and elbow, and Ben wondered how a boy could reach that age and not learn how to throw.

Stuart said, "There aren't any fly hatches at this time of year, are there, Ben?"

"I don't know. I doubt it, but the fish will still take a fly."

Meredith Stuart had removed her blouse and was now pulling down her slacks. She wore a peach-colored bikini. She had the body of a twenty-year-old: no stretch marks, no loose thigh or belly fat, no visible veins. She was long-legged, with a narrow waist and a round flare of hip, and small, firm breasts. She glanced at him.

Ben turned away. "I'll put some ice and a few beers and a couple of sandwiches in my creel."

"Do it," Stuart said. "Christ, what a day. I feel like a kid. Fish are waiting, Ben, let's get going."

They walked north along the water, around the bridge, and through some clawing brush at the base of an earthen bank. The river gradually increased in power and noise. Its surface was broken by chevron ripples and spinning, funnel-shaped whorls and iridescent cascades of foam. Water welled up and slid glassily over submerged rocks. Both men were sweating in the hard sunlight. Stuart breathed deeply, noisily. They reached the rapids, a fifty-yard chute filled with rocks, cresting waves, crashing foam; went on, jumped from stone to stone across the narrow creek, returned to the river, and entered the gorge.

The canyon walls abruptly narrowed just above the rapids; they were about one hundred feet apart here, and fairly steep, although not yet very high. The river, opaquely green, flowed smoothly and heavily between the walls. The banks were lined with tumbled rectangular blocks of age-blackened basalt. Above, on the desert, Ben had thought the world looked like glass; but down in the shadows everything appeared solid, hard, heavy, even the river. You could read the wall strata and look back a million years.

They paused to rest.

"I'll go first," Ben said. "But step carefully any-how—it's snakey in here."

"Rattlers?"

"Yeah."

"I don't like snakes," Stuart said. "I was bitten by a big diamondback when I was a kid. A huge son of a bitch, as long as your leg and just about as thick."

"What happened?"

"Nothing. He was dry, I guess. It scared me more than half to death, though. I near amputated my own leg cutting X's over the fang punctures."

Ben smiled.

"I never got sick. He was dry. I went back there every day for two weeks, found him, killed him, skinned and roasted him over a spit, and ate all I could."

"Why did you do that?"

Stuart shrugged. "That snake made me mad, Ben. I had a mean temper when I was a boy."

"So did I," Ben said. "An awful temper. I worked my old man over with an axe handle once."

"Jesus," Stuart said. "You did?"

"He beat the hell out of me when I was fourteen. I forgot what for—I probably deserved it. But he hurt me, I mean he really did hurt me, and I burned. Now, my old man didn't drink much, but when he did drink he went all the way. You know? Okay, so I waited seven months, and when he got drunk and passed out I hit him eight or ten times with the axe handle. He woke up sore and bruised and swollen—he could hardly walk for a week. He couldn't remember anything. I told him he'd fallen off the roof. I had a simply awful temper."

Stuart was grinning. "I guess you did, Ben. Did you ever tell your old man what you'd done?"

"Yeah, about six years afterward, when we both knew I could handle him if I had to."

"What did he say?"

"Said he'd never been able to figure out how a fall from a roof could stripe a man's body that way."

"I guess."

"Ready?" Ben said. "Let's go, then."

They cautiously picked their way over the confused jumble of rocks for two or three miles and stopped at the base of a long rapids. The walls became steeper and higher as they penetrated the gorge. The sky was now an incandescent blue ribbon overhead. There was sunlight on the upper third of the east wall, but the rest of the gorge was in shadow. The river crashed and hissed.

"This rapids runs up the canyon quite a ways," Ben said. "The fishing's not good in the rough water. We'll fish downstream from here. You go first, I'll follow about a hundred or so feet behind. I'll try any likely-looking spots you miss."

Stuart assembled his fly rod, test-whipped it a few times, leaned it against a rock, and opened his fly case. "What do you say, Ben?"

"Try the gray gnat."

Stuart tied the fly to the end of the tapered monofilament line. He moved a few yards away and began casting. Ben immediately saw that Stuart was an ex-

pert. He had a great wrist. It took a certain amount of
natural talent, touch, plus a thousand hours of practice to fly-cast with that kind of accuracy and economy of motion. This was a difficult place, too—you
had to be careful of the rocks, the bushy bank, and
the canyon wall. But Stuart did not even glance over
his shoulder. He flicked his wrist, retrieved the line,
flicked his wrist again, cast, released more line, cast
again, and dropped the fly just above a boulder and
let the current take it down. He tried the boulder
twice, and then made a long cast to the circular ed-
dies along the opposite bank. The tip of his rod made
a swishing sound. He took in some line, whipped the
rod, and dropped the fly on the smooth black water
above a hole. He moved downstream all the while,
trying all of the likely spots, swiftly working an area
of the river and then moving on. He had so mastered
technique that technique itself had vanished and left
only pure, clean function. Ben thought: The son of a
bitch fishes as if he's afraid the water's going to drain
out soon.

Ben waited until Stuart was well below him, and
then he began casting. He felt awkward after having
watched the Texan. Ben had always considered himself a pretty fair fly fisherman, but Stuart could thor-
oughly work a stretch of river in the time it took Ben
to make two or three good casts. The distance between them gradually increased.

Ben tried the silvery V-ripple in the center of the
river. He felt good, though a little resentful of Stuart's talent. It was a fine day. The water was swift
and cold and clear. It burst into foam against the big
black boulders that rose above the surface, curved

smoothly over the submerged rocks. A hawk, or maybe an eagle—it was much too high to tell—was a circling dot against the incredible sky. The sounds of the river resonated between the high rock walls, were amplified and altered; echoes created their own echoes. He could hear soft crashing noises, humming, splashes, bell-like tinkling, and a drumming which seemed to hover a hundred feet above the river. The water had a clean metallic smell, like steel shavings.

Stuart had vanished around a curve in the river. He fished like a machine. He's a technician, Ben thought. But he's good, damned good. A man who can do one thing very well can probably do other things well.

Ben got a strike; the tip of his rod dipped sharply, the shaft curved behind it, bent almost double, and he could feel the vibrant electricity of the fish transmitted up the line and rod to his wrist. But then the line went slack. Concentrate on the fishing, he told himself.

He fished for another hour without getting a strike, and then decided to catch up with Stuart. He found him a mile downstream, squatting at the river's edge and cleaning a big rainbow trout.

"Nice fish," Ben said.

"Yeah, he'll go about three pounds," Stuart said.

"That the only one?"

"No, I got two more in the creel. Not as big as this one, though. How'd you do, Ben?"

"I got shut out."

"Well, you were following me down. That can make a difference."

Ben sat on a rock and lit a cigarette.

Stuart scraped the trout's guts into the water, washed the fish, and placed it in his cruel. He straightened. "How about lunch now, Ben?"

"Sure." Ben got the sandwiches and two cans of beer out of his creel. He popped open the beer and slipped the metal tabs into his pocket.

"Look at that rock over yonder, Ben."

He looked: there were some crude figures of humans and animals chiseled into the basalt. "Petroglyphs," he said. "There are a lot of them down here."

"Are they old?"

"Yeah, pretty old."

"Are they worth any money, Ben?"

"I don't know. I suppose. But those big rocks would be hard to get out of here. Anyway, the rocks belong here, not on some Dallas lawn."

Stuart smiled. "How far up does this canyon run?"

"From where we parked the truck, for most of twenty, twenty-five miles."

"This is good country. Fine trout water, the mountains, some game. I like this country."

"It's going," Ben said.

"Sure, every place is going. The whole planet's going. Tell me something new."

"It's going because people have screwed up their cities so bad they can't live in them anymore. So they're moving out to screw up the country."

"I believe I'd like to buy some land around here, Ben."

"Is that so?"

"Do you know of any?"

"Not offhand, no."

Stuart was smiling at him. "I thought for sure you'd know of a good buy."

"I'm not a real estate agent."

"Still, Ben, I was sure you'd know of a good piece of land available at a good price."

"Nope."

"Someone who's in trouble, maybe, and has to sell."

"That's enough," Ben said.

"Aw, Ben, I was just kidding you."

"Do you want to fish some more?"

"Yes, Ben, but I'd like to finish my sandwich and my beer first."

"Okay."

"Don't get pissed, Ben. I was just joking you."

"I have a hard time slipping inside Texas humor."

"It's a fine day. Don't get mad. Really, Ben, I meant no harm."

"Okay."

"But, Ben, tell me, how did you get into so much financial trouble?"

"In just about every way one can."

"What are these lawsuits about? I know you're getting sued every which way, but I don't know exactly why and by who."

"Long story," Ben said.

"I know something about money, its uses and abuses. And I've been forced to learn a little about law. Ben, I might be able to give you some advice, maybe the names of some men who could help you."

"I'm being sued by the Indians—they claim they were never adequately compensated for the ranch lands. My lawyers tell me that they haven't got much of a case. And I'm being sued by a Spanish organization. The land was originally part of a big Spanish land grant, you see. They claim that they were cheated out of the land, that it's theirs. My lawyers don't think they have a case either. But the land titles are so miserably fouled up around here that the lawsuits could bounce around the courts for five years. More."

Stuart nodded. "The Spanish took the land away from the Indians, and the Anglos took the land away from the Spanish. Now they both want to take it back."

"It isn't that simple."

"Ben, how much do you owe the IRS?"

"Seventeen thousand dollars."

"Have they threatened to seize the ranch?"

"It has been mentioned as a possibility."

"How much do you owe the bank, Ben?"

"You know, don't you, that it's none of your business."

"I know. But I may be able to help you."

"I owe the bank about eight thousand dollars."

"Secured loans?"

"No, signature."

"Have they threatened to get a judgment against you?"

"It's been hinted."

"What else do you owe?"

"Bills—odds and ends. Big odds and ends, they total around fifty-five hundred."

"County taxes?"

"Yeah, that too. I've got to watch out there. Around here you can wake up some morning and hear the local sharpies outside the window auctioning off and buying your land, house, boots, and future. I don't have much confidence in a couple of the bank officers, either."

"Ben, you're in a deep hole."

"Tell me something I don't know."

"One of these days soon they're going to start shoveling dirt on your head."

"The money you're paying me will help a little."

"Pay your lawyers first. And give the IRS and the county some good-intentions tax money."

"Is that the advice you mentioned?"

"I want to think about it for a day or so, Ben. I want to get on the telephone and talk to some of my people in Dallas."

Ben regretted discussing his business with Stuart. He stood up.

"Ready?" Stuart asked.

"Let's fish," Ben said.

Eight

The jaguar screamed in rage and agony, then charged. Tom Stuart shouted hoarsely, threw his gun aside, turned and ran, crashing through the brush. Ben Pearce's shotgun misfired. He swore; then he too fled in shameless panic. The cat veered toward Meredith Stuart. It was only a few yards away. Peter stepped in front of his mother, coolly aimed his rifle, and fired. The cat, shot precisely between its eyes, died at his feet.

Peter turned and smiled sardonically. "Well, Mother," he said. "it seems that Father and Mr. Pearce had urgent business elsewhere."

That was just the right tone. In the fantasy Peter had seen himself wearing a bloody bandage wrapped around his forehead. He had not invented a reason for the bandage.

The western sky had remained smeared with rose and gold and crimson tints for ten minutes after the sun went down, and then the colors faded and it was night. A few stars appeared on the horizon. A chill came into the air. It was absolutely silent; when Peter held his breath he could hear nothing but the surge and ebb of his blood.

He sat on a tree stump at the far end of the orchard and looked over the indigo desert. Words which seemed to possess the power and reality of acts slipped into his consciousness. Holocaust. Fire, war, slavery. Blood. Ashes. Vengeance. Cataclysm.

He waited, but no more words came to him. He wondered if he should climb over the fence and walk out into the desert. There might be rattlesnakes out there, and coyotes—did coyotes attack humans? It seemed that everything did, from viruses so tiny they could be seen only through the most powerful electron microscopes, to elephants and whales. Still, it was tempting to go out into that moonlike landscape. An adventure. He had heard about people who had been picked up by flying saucers in the desert. They claimed to have been taken on journeys among the stars by gentle, brilliant creatures, gods. Peter did not wholly believe in flying saucers, he had doubts, but how could you know they didn't exist? There were many mysteries. There were truths which could not be comprehended within the limits of cheap, rational Western thought—flying saucers, Atlantis, the magic of the pyramids, auras, ESP (telepathy, telekinetic phenomena, clairvoyance, astral projection), reincarnation, the Bermuda triangle, astrology, the feats of yogis and fakirs, ghosts. He believed in those things more than he disbelieved.

Skeptics were narrow fools, cripples in the world to come. Like his father. Once his father had said something like "Peter, if you believe in everything now, someday you won't believe in anything." Another of the old man's stupid epigrams. He probably got it from the *Reader's Digest.* And that from a man who believed in the vicious Baptist god. Peter had replied (or maybe he had merely thought it later, he wasn't sure anymore): "If I believed only in what my senses told me was true I'd think the world was flat and the sun revolved around the earth." Had he really said that? Wait, yes. Now he remembered that his father's face had turned almost purplish red and he'd stuttered something about . . . what was it? He couldn't remember now. Maybe something about how that wasn't the same thing. That's what had happened. He'd turned red and angrily said, "But, Peter, that isn't the same thing." "Yes it is," Peter had coolly replied. Had that conversation really occurred?

Now Peter fantasized that his father was walking through the darkness toward him, a shadow among other shadows. He stopped a few feet away.

"Peter, I want to talk to you."

"Talk," Peter said. He looked out over the desert. The moon had climbed above the horizon now, and he could see the contours of land and the silvery shine of the sage. Moon-scaled mountains rose up into the stars.

"I don't like the way you've been treating your mother."

"I don't like the way *you've* been treating my mother," Peter said quietly.

The old man was silent for a time, and then in that rumbling hick drawl he said, "Get up on your feet. Look at me."

Peter slowly rose and turned. His father, massive, half in shadow and half in moonlight, was standing a few feet away.

"It's time we had it out, son. Defend yourself."

"No," Peter said calmly. "I do not believe in violence."

"I'm going to make you believe in it," and he slapped Peter with his open hand, snapping his head aside.

"Don't ever touch me again," Peter said coldly. "Not ever."

"Come on, chickenheart."

"Go away," Peter said softly. "We'll forget this."

"Shit," the old man said, and he slapped Peter again.

Peter swiftly coiled, became compact, and then he uncoiled with a shout of martial joy, delivering three deadly karate blows: a kick to his father's left knee (he could hear popping sounds as cartilage and ligaments tore), a stiff-fingered jab to the solar plexus, and then a tremendous edge-of-hand chop to the juncture of jaw and neck. The huge man collapsed loosely, silently, fell as if he had been hit between the eyes with a sledge. He lay chest-up on the ground. Moonlight pooled on his chest and trickled off onto the leaves.

And now Peter was chilled by despair: he had used the terrible power he had sworn to restrain; he had wiped out the icy discipline of a lifetime in a single angry moment. He, who sought only peace, had committed murder. And patricide—was there an uglier crime? And so now he must spend all of his remaining years in punishing his body and hubris: he would live alone in the mountains, exposed to the elements, eating berries and nuts and roots, gradually attaining absolution, until he finally reached a bitter, melancholy wisdom. . . .

Wait! His father wasn't dead, he moved now, groaned, opened his eyes—that last murderous karate chop had been a fraction off. And then Peter heard low, rumbling laughter.

"Jesus, boy, you got a kick like a mule and hands like bricks." His laughter was like a dog's stay-away-from-my-food growl.

"Sorry, Pa," Peter said.

"Well," his father said, "I don't mind meeting a man who's better than me, particularly if he's my own son." More laughter. "But you messed up my knee. You'll have to help me into the house."

Peter offered his hand; his father clasped it and was pulled erect.

"You're a whole lot stronger than you look, to pull me up like that."

"Let's go, Pa."

His father placed a heavy arm over Peter's shoulder, and they walked slowly through the orchard.

Peter was satisfied with the fantasy: it gave him his father's death (briefly) *and* reconciliation.

Now Peter walked beneath the trees, went through the gate and out into the big yard. It looked as if every light in the house were burning; the windows blazed and threw yellow squares and rectangles of light over the ground.

Peter crossed to the house, slid sideways along the wall until he came to a living room window. He slowly leaned out and looked into the room. It was bright and smoky inside. Mr. Pearce was sitting at one end of the couch, his father at the other end. Peter could hear the growl of their voices and understand a word here and there, but mostly it was as if they were speaking a foreign language. It was like watching a foreign film while deliberately ignoring the subtitles.

Peter withdrew from the window. He was obscurely excited. He had "spied" before, sometimes alone and sometimes with friends, and the blend of fear, guilt, sexuality, and power he experienced was electrifying—it had once put enough natural adrenaline in his system to temporarily cure an asthma attack.

To see while remaining unseen was a kind of power. It was a huge advantage. He thought it would be wonderful if you could make yourself invisible at will: you'd be able to go anywhere, do almost anything.

He leaned forward and looked through the window again. His mother sat between the window and a table lamp, and her hair formed a sparkling aureole around her profile. Peter thought his mother was prettier than any movie actress he'd ever seen.

His father looked huge, gross, vulgar. That much flesh was obscene. He was wearing his hat inside the house, and his stockinged feet rested on the coffee table. Big belly, jowls like a bulldog, small eyes that never stopped counting. A brutal gangster with fake *aw shucks* Western manners.

Mr. Pearce. Lazy, confused, nice enough on the surface, but Peter had seen signs of a mean streak in the man. He had liked Pearce at first; now he was not sure. Pearce was a killer, and obviously less sensitive than he seemed. He was intelligent, courteous, interesting to be with, but Peter had the feeling that something was missing in the man. There was a coldness there, a dead spot.

The evening was cold. The moon cast a pale surreal light over the landscape. A light breeze rattled the dry leaves in the tops of the cottonwoods.

The dogs barked and growled furiously as he passed the corner of the shed. He went on, following the left-curving path through the high weeds to the cemetery gate. He hesitated, then went through. He had the feeling that the dead were alert to his trespass, that if he wanted he could snap his fingers and they would claw their way out of the graves and dance for him.

Moonlight angled in from the southwest and cast tree branches and askew shadows of crosses and monuments over the weedy ground. The shadows of the fence spears stretched toward him, pierced his ankles. He shifted until the dark spears bent at right angles against his chest. He raised his arms high and crossed his wrists: Saint Anthony, struck by arrows. He lowered his arms, extended them horizontally: Christ. Father, why hast Thou forsaken me?

Wind gusted, spinning the leaves overhead and sending confused patterns of light and shadow over the ground.

Peter sat on one of the marble monuments. His feet rested on the grave. There's someone down there, he thought. Green, rotten, maggoty, stinking, vile. And someday I'll be in a hole like that: green, rotten, maggoty, stinking, vile.

"Oh, dear God!" Peter said huskily, and he started to cry. He didn't know why he was crying. He felt nothing. Maybe even his pain was a reflex. He had difficulty these days separating what he actually felt from what he only expected himself to feel. He observed himself suffering and was not convinced.

He wept and sobbed helplessly, not believing in his pain. And all the while he felt that he was being lost, that what remained of his true self was dissipating like smoke. He was aware of losing substance, turning into a ghost. It was sad, very sad, but it had very little to do with him.

He left the cemetery. The dogs barked at him again. They barked, snarled, yapped, hurled themselves against the wire screen. He walked to the fence, kneeled, offered his hand so the dogs could smell him and understand that he was a sad, good, gentle boy.

The moon was reflected in their eyes, gleamed on their wet teeth. Peter pressed the back of his hand against the wire; a sacrifice to their savagery. Gradually, all of the dogs but one settled down, became sullen; barks turned to low growls, to faint whimpers, finally to silence. The smallest of them, a black-and-white, piglike creature, continued to snarl and yap.

Peter offered his hand. "It's okay," he crooned. "I'm your friend, it's okay, fella." Did this animal sense the evil in him?

The dog advanced slowly, snarling, and then it suddenly leaped forward and slashed at Peter's hand. Its teeth clicked against the wire.

Peter jerked his hand back, looked down, touched it. The dog had not bitten him.

"Good boy, good fella," Peter crooned.

The little dog snarled, barked, moved forward quickly, and then retreated.

Peter turned and started walking toward the house.

Nine

*B*en dreamed that he was dead. His corpse was lying supine in the shade of a grove of cottonwoods (was it the grove by the family cemetery?).
His torso had been ripped open from throat to crotch,
and some cats—the leopard, the jaguar, the two
mountain lions, and many others—were devouring
his insides. A fragment of consciousness survived
death, and it watched from a distance as they dipped
their neat cat heads into the wound and tore out coils
of bluish-pink intestine, the liver, kidneys, stomach,
heart and lungs. They were hungry and yet fastidious,
cat delicate. Ruby-clear drops of blood dripped like
tears from the tips of their whiskers. Every now and
then one would pause to stare suspiciously into space
before bending to lick the blood from its paw. Ben
could smell the cats. He could hear the wheezy rattle

of their purring. And then he noticed that there were other cats dozing in the hard sunlight beyond the trees. Hundreds of cats: lions, tigers, leopards, cheetahs, margays, cougars, bobcats, lynx, jaguars, jaguarundis, domestic cats—all of them fat-bellied and sleepy. Their eyes were half-lidded. They yawned. They twitched their whiskers and flicked their tails to drive off the flies. And Ben saw that *more* cats were slowly walking toward his corpse, moving stiff-spined and slope-shouldered across the sunburned plains.

He sat up on the edge of his bed. It was after six o'clock; the windows were beginning to glow palely in the darkness of his room. He could still smell the cats. And he could hear the wet sounds they made while eating.

Am I hung over this morning? No, no, I didn't drink after dinner, and I went to bed early. Christ, that was a dream.

Ben got dressed and quietly walked through the house to the kitchen. He put a pot of coffee on the stove. He sat down at the table.

The jaguar today. She was a fine-looking, powerful animal. He hoped the kid would be able to kill her cleanly. There was a chance. Peter had seen how easy it could be the day before, when his mother shot the mountain lion. Jesus, she was cold. It meant nothing to her. She hadn't shown any more emotion than if she were popping clay birds at a country-club trap shoot.

He got up, poured a mugful of coffee, added cream and sugar, lit a cigarette, and went outside. An ancient cold morning, beginning to turn blue now. Vertiginous space, a hard geometrical landscape, a smell of ice and earth and dead fires. Ravens were quarreling in the cottonwood trees. Beyond the crooked spears and crosses of the cemetery, a half-dozen erect prairie dogs were holding a sunrise prayer meeting.

Ben sipped his coffee, inhaled from the cigarette. He could see a pinpoint of light—Venus. It was always good to be outdoors at this hour. Nothing mattered beyond the simple fact that you were still sucking air into your lungs. Later in the day existence would begin to intrude upon life.

The dogs were barking hysterically from their kennel behind the shed. Ben started that way to see what was exciting them. He was halfway across the yard when Peter walked around the corner of the building. He moved slowly, his shoulders rounded, hands in pockets, looking down at the ground. He looked vaguely guilty, as always. Ben watched him, thinking that the boy needed real guilt, a hellfire sin; no one can suffer as miserably as the innocent.

"Good morning, Peter."

The boy stopped abruptly, jerked up his head. "What? Oh, good morning, Mr. Pearce."

"Call me Ben."

"I was just . . ." He shook his head. "The dogs don't like me," he said.

"They're just dogs, Peter."

"They hate me."

"They're dogs, not your jury."

"I've heard that dogs have a kind of instinct about people."

Ben smiled. "A dog will bite the hand of a saint

and lick the hand of the devil, if the devil throws him a bone every now and then."

"I don't know." The boy was even paler than usual this morning, and he had difficulty breathing because of his asthma.

"You're a screwed-up kid if you go around soliciting the endorsement of dogs."

Peter smiled faintly, nodded.

"There's coffee in the kitchen if you want some," Ben said.

Peter shook his head.

"Listen, kid, how do you expect to go running around the mountains today with that asthma of yours?"

He shrugged.

"You can hardly breathe now."

"I'm okay."

"You sound like you're choking to death on your own spit. Look, you don't want to kill that cat— here's your exit."

He shook his head. "No, Mr. Pearce, I'm going to do it."

"What about your asthma?"

"My mother will give me an injection of Adrenalin."

"All right, then."

"I have to do this, Mr. Pearce."

"My other name is Ben. Why do you have to do it?"

"To show my father that I can."

"And what if you fail?"

"I won't fail. I can't."

"Okay," Ben said. He sipped his coffee; it was getting cold.

"I'll tell you what I'm going to do, Mr. Pearce," the boy said. He was looking directly into Ben's eyes now. His big hands were at his sides, clenched into fists. "I'm going to shoot that jaguar. I'm going to kill him the way my father wants me to. And then when we get back here, I'm going to invite my father out into that orchard over there. Just him and me. Do you understand?" His eyes were bright, fevered.

"No, I'm not sure I do understand, Peter."

"Mr. Pearce, I'm going to kill that jaguar and then I'm going to challenge my father to a fistfight."

"Okay. But you know your old man will knock the hell out of you."

"Maybe so, maybe not. But I'll fight bravely."

Ben threw his remaining coffee out onto the ground.

"I'll kill that poor cat, I'll fight my father—and then he'll know that I'm not a coward, that I can be his kind of man, but I can be my own kind, too."

Ben shook his head.

"I'll be free."

"He'll just demand more of you. He'll raise the stakes."

The boy started to speak, hesitated, then shook his head when the words wouldn't come.

"It won't work, Peter."

"Why not?"

"You aren't ready. It isn't settled in your mind yet. A boy who's anxious for the good opinion of dogs isn't ready to fight his father."

"You believe I'll fail," he said. His stance and his eyes were aggressive.

"I hope you take the jaguar out with one clean, perfect shot. I hope you knock your old man on his ass."

"You hope, but you don't expect it."

"No."

"But why *not*?"

"Come on, kid, let's go in the house and get some breakfast."

"Why not?"

"You aren't ready, Peter. You want to fail as much as you want to succeed. You can't win. Later, maybe. I've been down the same road, I know."

"Shitkicker psychology," Peter said softly, furiously. "I thought you were different," he said contemptuously. "But you aren't, you're just like my old man. Just another redneck."

Ben turned and started walking toward the shed.

"Going to kick the dogs around, Mr. Pearce?" Peter called mockingly.

Ben halted, turned. "No, but I'm not going to beg for their approval, either." He resumed walking.

"Tell me about hard times," Peter called. "Tell me about how you had to work twelve hours a day when you were my age."

I did, Ben thought.

Peter laughed and then coughed. "Tell me about walking four miles to school in blizzards when you were my age!"

Six miles there and six miles back, you supercilious punk.

"Tell me I've had it too soft, Mr. Pearce!"

You have, kid, you've had it much too easy.

"You stink, Pearce!" the boy screamed.

Ben turned the corner of the shed and stood in front of the kennel. The dogs whined and leaped against the wire.

"You are excellent judges of character," Ben said.

I dug fence post holes all day in the hot sun when I was that kid's age. I strung wire. I shoveled out irrigation ditches. I castrated calves, branded steers. I broke horses. I put up hay. I shot deer and turkey and grouse for the table. I cut timber. I plowed. I rode herd. I butchered. I worked summer and winter, ninety-five degrees in the shade or thirty degrees below zero. I salted and smoked and cured. I tanned hides. I made soap out of lye and animal fat. I made my own apple cider and got drunk on it. I'd had three or four broken bones and a couple of concussions by the time I was that boy's age. I'd been drunk, I'd known women, I had swung on my father by the time I was fifteen. My father was a halfway rich man in those days but I still had to work like a barefoot bean-hungry peon. And I had to study, too. And somehow there was still time for play. I was a man when I was fifteen. Tom Stuart is a mean, bullying prick, but he's a man. His son is no good; Stuart ought to write him off.

"Do you love me?" Ben asked the dogs.

These are different times, bad times. Bad times. It isn't all the kid's fault. I like him at moments. He's bright, and he has a nice, dry sense of humor on any subject that doesn't concern himself. He's cynical, but not where cynicism could do him any good. What the hell, I like the boy okay. It isn't all his fault. It's the times. And his father is a Dallas fascist and his mother is a sexy witch. I wish the kid would simply say, "No, I will not kill the jaguar." Either that or go out and do the job right.

The odd thing was it, it would be good for Peter to kill the cat if he did it cleanly. It would give him the crime he so desperately needed; he was strangling on his own concept of virtue. It would earn him his father's respect, and therefore a small piece of self-respect as well. It would loosen the chain his mother had around his neck.

"Shitkicker psychology," Ben said furiously. "Is a redneck like me worthy of your affection?" he asked the dogs.

The jaguar today, the leopard tomorrow. A buffalo and an antelope the day after, if Stuart wants them. And maybe Stuart will want to kill the female mountain lion with his bow. Four days at the most. I can stand them for four more days.

They were the only people Ben had ever met who made him feel like a pimp.

Tom Stuart was wearing a holstered .357 Magnum revolver around his waist when he came out of the house. He walked across the frozen yard toward Ben. He held his arms well away from his body; he breathed smoke. He was big and slow and sleepy-looking. Ben thought he moved with the same kind of slowness as all fast men, athletes, do: it seemed as if they were always saving themselves for the crucial ten or fifteen seconds of violent action to come. They were slow, lazy, and then they exploded.

"Morning, Ben," Stuart said.

"Morning. I asked you not to carry a gun on these hunts."

"You said rifle, Ben. This is a sidearm."

"Take it off."

"Now, Ben, are you going to argue with old Tom again this morning?" The words hummed in his throat and came out slurred, all the consonantal edges worn smooth.

"Please leave the revolver here," Ben said.

Stuart smiled. "You're a mule, Ben. A thick-skulled, humpbacked mule."

"I know," he said. And he thought, Jesus, every encounter with a Stuart is a wearying, unrelenting defensive battle to hold on to your pride and self-respect—they have to reduce you in order to enlarge themselves.

"You can kick a mule or sweet-talk him," Stuart said.

"Your choice."

"Now, Ben, hear me—this gun will stay holstered until it's *needed*."

"It won't be needed."

"You aren't listening, Ben. I want you to listen. No, goddamn it, don't talk—listen closely just this once. You're invariably hearing but you're never *listening*. Now, Ben, I like this place. This is a good place. There's still some game here, and good trout water, and mountains and pure air. I like it here. Mere and Peter like it here. I've got lots of money, more than I can ever spend, and I want a place away from the city. I'll spend maybe half of the time in the city and half here. I want—Listen to me, Ben! Talk later, okay? Now I want a place. This place. Not all of it, Ben, fifty percent."

Ben shook his head. "No. Forget it."

"Will you listen? I like you. Now, you're in cold trouble, you're going to lose everything in a year or eighteen months. I know, Ben, my accountants told me. I phoned them and they called me back. My accountants know money like a squirrel knows trees. You told me yourself the paper you got out. The IRS has you by one ball and the banks have your other one. If you had more balls there'd be someone there to squeeze them—the land-grant Chicanos, the Indians, the local sharpies. You got debts, Ben, lawsuits, liens soon—and no money coming in or likely to come in except for these hunts you're running. How long can that last?"

"I've listened," Ben said.

"I'm not finished."

"You'd eat me alive," Ben said.

"I'm not asking for fifty-one percent, Ben—just fifty."

"Your money and your lawyers and accountants would have me barefoot on the streets in fifteen months."

"Ben, I'm a generous man."

"I've noticed that people most often brag about the virtue they fail to possess."

Stuart grinned. "I'm generous to a point."

"I'm gullible to a point."

"Ben, I can see that you believe I'm trying to screw you over. That's not true, believe me. I'm offering to save your land. One hundred percent of nothing is still nothing. Fifty percent of something is *something*, Ben. I can go partners with you now, or I can wait a year and go head-up against the local hustlers at auction."

"Okay," Ben said.

"Now wait, Ben. I wouldn't bother you. I'd build my home three, four miles from here, up where you can smell pine. I wouldn't bother you at all. I wouldn't touch the land, I wouldn't try to make a dollar off of it—why would I foul my own nest? Ben, we could burn off the sage, the grass might come back. We wouldn't exploit the land, Ben, we'd let it go back to what it was, we'd turn it into a kind of park. We could have mule deer, antelope out there. And maybe elk when they come down out of the high country in winter. And hell—why not?—some coyotes and big cats to keep the herds healthy. And cover for birds, pheasant, quail, grouse. Do you see what I'm talking about, Ben? I want the same thing that you want. And I can *get* it for us."

"It wouldn't work."

"I like you, Ben, Christ knows why. No, I know why—because you remind me of the boys I used to run with when I was a boy. We were mean, hard, wild boys, Ben, but honest. Bad boys, people would say now, but we had our code. You were like that, weren't you? You remind me of my kid brother. Shit yes, that's it—you're like Danny. He was killed in Korea. But that's neither here nor there. Ben, I'm making you a straight and square offer. Now what do you say?"

"It wouldn't work."

"Will you think about it?"

"No."

"You're just like Danny," Stuart said, shaking his head. "If a man was dying of thirst you wouldn't spit on him."

"Sure I would," Ben said.

Stuart laughed silently.

"Put up the gun now, will you?"

"Okay, Ben, I'll let you win the small ones. But you'll accept my offer in the end, because you have no choice." Stuart turned and started back toward the house.

"Stuart," Ben said.

He stopped and turned.

Ben approached him. "I was talking to your son this morning."

Stuart waited.

"His asthma is very bad. The boy can hardly breathe."

"Meredith will give him an injection of Adrenalin."

"He's very confused and anxious. He's half crazy with anxiety, he doesn't know which way to jump. Take the pressure off him."

"How?"

"He doesn't want to kill the jaguar."

"He hasn't told me that."

"It's true. And you know it's true."

"Ben, all he has to do is tell me."

"He won't."

"He's got to make *decisions*, Ben. He's got to act."

"He isn't ready."

Stuart was silent for a time; then he said: "Ben, I know you think I'm too hard on Peter, that I demand too much. But he has to be pushed, and *now*. Peter has to find out what's inside of him, he's got to start knowing himself. He won't ever try anything, he won't test himself. This world is going to eat him alive unless he grows strong."

"You'll break him."

Stuart nodded slowly. "Maybe. I hope not, but maybe. The boy was raised under a lot of stress, Ben. It made him weak. All I can see is maybe stress can cure what stress has made. I don't see another way."

"All right," Ben said.

"He's at the age when a boy has to test himself, learn his strengths and limits. It's true, Ben, and you know it. Because if Peter doesn't start learning now, he never will. And he'll be dead by the time he's twenty-five—he'll take an overdose of drugs, or he'll blow out his brains, or someone'll murder him. Peter's a natural victim now, he's begging to be abused, and there are millions of people who'll sense that and accommodate him if they get the chance. Do you understand all this, Ben?"

"No."

"But you do understand, Ben, don't lie."

The thing was, Ben did understand.

Peter's asthma was much worse during the truck ride into the foothills. His breathing was rapid; there was a crackling sound in his exhalations, and his inhalations were throaty gasps, a desperate sucking of air. Ben parked the truck and turned off the ignition. They sat quietly for a time, and then quietly, fearfully, the boy said, "Mother, I can't—I can't *breathe*, Mother."

They all got out of the truck. Meredith Stuart's

face was a smooth mask. Without hurrying, she reached into her shoulder bag and withdrew a clear plastic box which contained disposable hypodermic syringes and half a dozen plastic ampules.

The boy was sitting on the ground now, his elbows resting on his raised knees, his head lowered and cupped in his palms. His chest heaved; air hissed and crackled deep in his throat.

Tom Stuart looked away, up toward the high country.

Meredith Stuart removed a small bottle of alcohol and a box of cotton from her bag.

Ben could hear the whining of the dogs in the camper shell.

Meredith took her son's hand, gently extended his arm, and then rubbed alcohol-soaked cotton on his forearm.

"Intravenous, Mother," Peter gasped.

"No, dear, it's so difficult to find your veins." She was very cool and precise.

"Intramuscular then, but please hurry."

She inserted the ampule into the syringe, dipped the needle into alcohol, squeezed out a few drops of the clear fluid, and then leaned forward and slowly drove the needle at an angle into the muscle of Peter's forearm.

Ten

*B*en turned and walked the few yards to where Stuart was standing. "How long does it take for that stuff to work?" he asked.

"Why? Are we running short of time?"

"We've got a half-hour."

"No problem, Ben. The boy'll be breathing easy soon."

"I can call it off."

"Now why in the world would you want to do something like that?"

"Bernard and I have a signal—if I fire off a gun three times it means he shouldn't release the cat."

"Ben, there's no need. I *told* you that Peter will be just fine as soon as that Adrenalin gets to working."

"Look," Ben said, "I don't understand why—" He heard his voice rising, and twisted around and glanced over his shoulder. Peter was still sitting hunched over on the ground; his head was lowered, his eyes were closed, and his posture and forced breathing suggested that he had to consciously will each inhalation and exhalation. His mother was kneeling next to him, crooning softly and stroking his hair.

"Let's take a short walk," Ben said.

They walked thirty yards away, stopped, and faced each other. Stuart's cheeks were puffed out, and his eyes were half-lidded: it was his harassed *am I going to have to listen to more of your crap* look.

"Peter's sick," Ben said.

Stuart let his cheeks deflate, the air hissing between his teeth.

"Why does he need Adrenalin?" Ben asked.

"It's a stimulant."

"I know that. What does it stimulate? His heart?"

"His heart, yes. Respiration. His whole system, I guess. It does whatever natural adrenaline does."

"What would have happened if your wife hadn't been carrying the Adrenalin today?"

"She usually does carry it. Peter carries it himself when he's away from home."

"He gives himself shots?"

"If he has to."

"Okay, but what would happen if he had an attack like this and there was no Adrenalin?"

"Ben, just what is your point?"

"Your son is ill."

"And he has just received medication."

"Christ, man, he sounds like he's dying."

Stuart, smiling crookedly, shook his head, removed

his Stetson with one hand and scratched behind an ear with the other, replaced the hat, and tugged at the brim. He puffed up his cheeks again and let the air slowly hiss out.

"We're at nearly seventy-five hundred feet here," Ben said. "The air's thin, and we'll be going higher, moving fast. What's going to happen?"

"Ben—"

"It's too much for him now. Let's wait a day or two, until this attack passes."

"Ben," Stuart drawled, "do you really think that Mere and I are sending that boy up into the hills to *die*?"

"Of course not, but—"

"But no buts, Ben. I've listened to you once again. Now you just listen to me just a second."

"Look, Stuart—"

"Why do I always have to plead for your attention, Ben? Now you don't know anything about Peter's asthma, do you? I've lived with it. I'm his father, Ben, I know what he can do and what he can't do. So does Meredith. Do you believe his mother would send him off into the mountains if there was any real danger? Peter is *not* an invalid. No way. He's in a funk about killing this cat, that's the truth, and that's why he's had a bad attack at this particular time. I know it. Mere knows it. Even Peter knows it. There's a psychological aspect to asthma, you know."

"Okay," Ben said.

"Peter isn't an invalid. He can do."

"All right," Ben said.

"He *will* do. Down deep where it counts, Peter is strong. We've got to get him to tap that strength."

"We'd better go back and get ready," Ben said.

"Don't give me that goofy walleyed stare of yours, Ben. You're a pushy guy sometimes. Go easy."

"Go easy yourself," Ben said angrily.

"Now we're going to walk back there and we're going to talk to Peter and Mere. You're going to see that Peter isn't wheezing and dying. And you'll find that Peter can run with you in the hills. Hell, man, he's not yet sixteen and you're forty—you'll be begging for mercy when he gets his wind."

Stuart turned and started walking slowly back toward the truck. Small puffs of dust erupted at his heels. His back was huge. He had a slouchy, spring-kneed walk now, the lazy stride of a horseman who has been deprived of his mount. Stuart's walk, like his drawl and the set of his shoulders and the rumble in his voice, was subtly altered to fit each new occasion.

Ben walked toward the truck. Peter and his mother were standing now. Stuart, the Stetson tilted back on his head, was slouched against the right front fender.

"Here comes the doctor now," Stuart was saying. "Say 'ah' for the doctor, folks."

"We've got about twenty-five minutes," Ben said.

"I'm okay, Mr. Pearce, honest," Peter said.

"I'm sure you are, Peter. Your father has just convinced me that asthma is a trivial affliction. Get the rifle. Safety on and no cartridge in the chamber."

"I feel much better now, really. And when we go after the jaguar, when I get, you know, excited, well, my body will produce some natural adrenaline. I'll be fine."

"Okay, Peter." Ben thought the boy did look and

sound much better. He was pale, there was a fevered burning in his eyes, and still a wheezy rattle in his breathing, but he was on his feet now and seemed eager to begin the hunt.

Stuart had gone around to the truck cabin, and now he returned with the rifle. He removed the clip, slid back the bolt, glanced down into the chamber, slammed the bolt closed, and reinserted the clip. He gave the rifle to his son.

"Safety's on, chamber's empty," Stuart said.

Peter nodded.

Stuart grinned and slapped his son roughly on the shoulder. "Piece of cake," he said jovially. "Relax, you'll be just fine. I expect to see a dead cat within the hour. Just think about how much pure fun it's going to be to sit in front of the fire tonight with a glass of brandy, talking about this day and how you bagged your cat."

Peter glanced at his mother. She smiled.

"Tell you what, boy," Stuart went on. "You kill this jaguar with a little style—and I know you will— and I'll buy you a goddamned Jaguar *automobile*. We'll go down to the showroom as soon as we get back to Dallas and you pick out your car. How's that?"

Peter nodded jerkily.

"A Jaguar for a jaguar. It'll be easy, you'll see."

Stuart stuck out his hand. Peter flinched slightly, then shifted the rifle to his left hand and extended his right.

All wrong, Ben thought, Stuart's handling this all wrong. It should be approached casually, offhand— good luck, bust that cat—but the stakes are being

made too high: an expensive automobile, companion-
ship by the fire, a handclasp, the reward of complete
approval.

"Okay," Ben said. "We've got some time until
Bernard releases the jaguar. Peter and I can get
started now. We'll walk easy and gain some altitude.
Tom, when you hear the dogs start trying to break out
of the camper that will mean they've heard the whistle. Open the doors and let them go."

"I'm coming along," Stuart said.

"Sure. Just release the dogs at nine and follow
them."

Ben looked at Meredith. She had wandered a few
yards away and was gazing dreamily up toward the
mountains. She had isolated herself again, gone into
that euphoric state that in some obscure way reminded Ben of death. Now, as he watched, she lifted
her chin, closed her eyes, and smiled at the sun.

Ben got his shotgun from the truck. "Let's go, Peter," he said.

They walked northeast across the desert.

"Relax," Ben said. "You don't have to hold the rifle at 'present arms.' This isn't a military inspection."

Peter lowered the rifle a few degrees.

"You're trying to strangle that rifle. Hold it easy,
in one hand. Find the balance point and carry it about
the same way you'd carry a lunch pail or briefcase.
It's heavier, that's all. Relax."

The boy awkwardly changed to a one-handed grip.

"That's it," Ben said, although it wasn't "it" at all;
Peter's knuckles were white from pressure.

The sun was warmer now, and it evoked the tart

scents of dust and sage and juniper. There were deer tracks in the reddish soil.

"How are the lungs?" Ben asked.

"I'm okay," he answered sullenly.

"There's an arroyo up ahead that'll give us easy access to the mountains. Water takes the easiest way downhill, and it will generally show you the easiest way uphill, too. There's no water there now, of course, though it was a stream a long time ago. It's still a main conduit of the mountain drainage system when there's a heavy rain or when the snows melt."

The boy was silent.

"We won't have to fight trees or brush, either. The arroyo floods often enough so that not much grows in it."

Peter stopped and coughed violently for a moment, spit out the phlegm, and resumed walking.

"With an early start and going easy this way, we can gain some altitude before the jaguar is released. A few hundred feet of altitude and a mile of penetration will help. But I also figured that it might be a fair idea to leave your parents behind. You can kill the jaguar by yourself, without them staring over your shoulders. What do you think?"

Peter cleared his throat again, spit. "I *want* them to see it."

"All right. It just seemed to me that if you're going to do this at all you should do it for yourself."

"I wouldn't do it for myself."

"You wouldn't, huh?"

"No way. They have to be there."

"Well, if nothing goes wrong we can wait until they catch up with us."

"I don't think you understand what this means to me, Mr. Pearce."

"It means a nice car."

"Fuck the car."

"Good."

"I won't accept the car."

"I'm glad to hear that."

"The car's a bribe."

"There are other bribes involved too, Peter. Sort them out."

The arroyo was about seven feet deep and twice that width where they entered it; gradually it became narrower and shallower as it twisted up into the hills. Forested slopes rose steeply on either side. Here and there small feeder arroyos angled in through gaps in the hills. It was easy going. The angle of ascent was rarely more than twenty-five degrees. The soil was firm. There were no obstructions.

As they walked, Ben explained what the bed would look like when filled with water: "Here a series of falls pouring over water-smoothed boulders; here in this level stretch a deep and fairly calm pool; and now here, in the steep section, white water, rapids. Imagine the rush, the noise. And notice how water has rounded and smoothed the rocks and ground hard stone into sand. It's like the sand on a beach, isn't it? Up ahead we'll pass between a couple of ten-foot-high rock walls. You'll be able to stretch your arms out and touch the walls on either side. The passage is short, and beneath the sand bed you'll find more rock—think of it, water slowly carved out tons of rock, chiseled out a deep U in a massive boulder. It was a natural dam at one time. Water went over the top at first, I suppose, found flaws here and there, cracks probably, and just went on and grain by grain, chip by chip, carved out a passage. Makes you think, doesn't it, Peter? Water and rock. Time. Death. This area here was once part of a great inland sea, I've heard. Time ticking away over billions of years. Water and rock. Water has all the time it needs. The whole planet's a kind of ruin. When I was a kid I thought about becoming a geologist so that I could read the ruin the way you'd read a book."

Peter was having difficulty breathing. Ben stopped occasionally to point something out, talk about it, giving the boy a chance to rest.

They passed between the rock walls. "Look at the strata of the rock, Peter. Now I don't know, but it seems to me that you can roughly calculate when there were really wet periods and when there were dry. Like reading the growth rings on a tree trunk. It's very seldom that water runs through here nowadays. But it'll come back. Water will go back to work here. Water has time. Not even granite can stand up against water. Like, maybe, water is the unstoppable force and rock is the immovable object. Except it moves. Water breaks it down into grains and carries it away."

At a few minutes before nine o'clock, Ben and Peter left the arroyo and climbed a steep, wooded hill to the top.

"Let's sit down here for a while," Ben said. "The cat will probably come in this direction. This way, but a little higher. They usually do."

Peter propped his rifle against a tree, coughed and spit again, and then sat down on a flat rock. There was a dry crackling in his exhalations, like the sound of cellophane being crumpled.

"You doing okay?" Ben asked.

The boy nodded.

"It's about nine. We'll hear the dogs soon. Did you bring along any more Adrenalin?"

"I'm *okay*!" Peter said angrily.

"We gained some height," Ben said. "You see that tree? It's a Douglas fir. Their real growth zone is a little higher, but you run into some strays down here. Most of these other trees are ponderosa pine and blue spruce. Here, I'll show you the difference in their cones—"

"Mr. Pearce," the boy interrupted.

Ben looked at him.

"Are you trying to distract me from the jaguar?"

Ben smiled. "Why, yes, I am."

"It won't work."

"Okay."

"Because that's all I can think about now, the cat."

"I can understand that."

"I'm sorry, but I don't think I heard a single word you said down below. I don't know what you were saying. I wasn't listening."

"I was hardly listening to myself," Ben said.

"I'm just scared. Man, I tell you, *I am scared*."

"The cat won't hurt you. I'll see to that."

"I'm not afraid of being *hurt*," Peter said. "You don't understand at all."

"Well, there's nothing else worth being scared about. You'll kill the cat cleanly or you won't. It's best that you make a good shot, but it isn't any kind of tragedy if you don't. No more important to your life than if you dropped a pass in the end zone, if you played football, or getting drunk and making a fool of yourself at a prom. It doesn't matter much. At your age some things seem—Listen, the dogs are loose now."

Peter cocked his head, listened. His hands, which had been loosely clasped on his knees, began to writhe.

Ben lit a cigarette. "We've got a little time yet. The jaguar is south of us, coming this way, I hope."

"Can I put a bullet into the chamber now?"

"No, hell no. We've got some running to do yet."

"I'd feel better if the rifle was ready to shoot."

"Well, I wouldn't. Just leave it for now."

They were quiet for a time, and then Ben stood up. It sounded as though the dogs, in just a few minutes, had gained as much altitude as he and Peter had in their twenty-minute hike. The dogs were about due south of them now and going hard, still climbing. Ben hoped that the jaguar would not be able to run for long. The cat was soft, fat and soft, immature— maybe they would be lucky today and get a quick shot.

"Damn," Peter said in a husky voice. "Damn, damn, damn."

Ben turned. The boy was pounding the heel of his fist onto his right thigh. His arm rose, flexed, and fell. His eyes were pressed shut and his teeth were locked. And each time he struck his leg he said "Damn!"—"Damn, damn, damn, damn"—his arm rising and falling.

"Cut it out," Ben said. "The dogs are coming this way."

Peter's eyes were lensed with tears.

"It's about how I figured. The cat's running this way, but he's higher than this. We'll have to climb some."

The boy averted his eyes. Nodded.

"Get your rifle. We'll start now."

They had luck: the jaguar was treed within a half mile of where they had waited. Ben jogged easily and walked, jogged and walked. The boy was able to maintain the pace, but toward the end he was staggering, weaving like a drunk through the trees, and his breathing sounded like the rapid tearing of fabric.

Last winter or the winter before, a big fir tree had fallen and its upper end had caught in the branches of another tree. Now, roots exposed, bare of branches, it slanted upward at a forty-five-degree angle. The jaguar had climbed halfway up the trunk, turned, and now lay on her belly and stared down at the frantically barking dogs. Her sides heaved. Her mouth was open, and her tongue spilled out of the side of her mouth. She did not appear to be fearful or angry; she lifted her head and stared directly at Ben for at least ten seconds, then half yawned and turned to stare again at the dogs.

"Take off the safety and kick a cartridge into the chamber," Ben said.

The boy worked the bolt.

"Take it easy for a minute now. Catch your breath."

Peter nodded. His lower lip was bleeding; he must have bitten it while running.

Ben waited until Peter was breathing more freely, and then said, "Are you ready?"

"No, not yet."

"Peter, the jaguar isn't going to wait all morning."

"My mother and father aren't here."

"Don't be stupid. Shoot the cat."

Peter slowly shook his head.

"Look, I know how you feel about this. Give me the rifle. I'll kill the cat and we'll tell your parents that you did it."

"No."

"Okay. But if that cat starts to come down from there I'm going to shoot her. And I'll keep your old man's money."

The boy was crying soundlessly now. He wiped the tears away with the back of his left hand. His skin was flushed and sweaty; his eyes burned hotly; he shivered. He looked as though he were being consumed by an inner conflagration, his health burning up in a single prolonged flash.

Finally the Stuarts, breathing heavily, came toward them.

"Thanks for waiting, Ben," Stuart called.

"It wasn't my idea," Ben said. "Stay back now, will you?"

Stuart kept walking and moved next to his son.

"I told you how I work these hunts," Ben said. "I asked you to stay away. You and your wife will have to move back now."

Stuart ignored him. "You've got a good, clear shot, Peter."

"She's just laying up there," the boy said.

"Smooth and easy," Stuart said. "Take her now."

"Will you please get the hell out of here?" Ben said.

The boy licked the blood off his lip.

"All right, son."

Peter sobbed, moaned softly.

The cat slowly raised up, stood lightly balanced on the slanting tree.

"Stuart," Ben said, "that cat is getting ready to come down and kill about three of my dogs."

"Peter," Stuart said. "For Christ's sake, shoot the animal."

"She's going to come down, goddamn it," Ben said.

"Peter?" Meredith Stuart said softly. A question, a demand, a rebuke, a promise.

The boy raised the rifle, closed his eyes, and pulled the trigger.

A small branch twenty feet above the jaguar exploded into fragments.

Peter, his eyes still closed, worked the bolt, shot, worked the bolt, shot, his body revolving and the rifle lifting until he was aiming directly up at the sky. He kept working the bolt and pulling the trigger after the magazine was empty.

Tom Stuart stepped forward and snatched the rifle away from his son. He waited until Peter opened his eyes, and then he quietly said, "I quit on you, Peter. Be what you want. Be a faggot. I quit."

The jaguar dropped down off the tree. All of the dogs except the Airedale scattered. Ben quickly aimed and fired both barrels of his shotgun. The cat screamed and began biting and clawing at her entrails, unraveling them, spinning around very quickly at first and then slower and slower, until her eyes glazed and she could no longer stand. She settled into the dust with a whine. Pink blood frothed around her mouth. Ben had killed the Airedale with the same shot.

Peter turned and started walking down the hill. His mother followed.

"Go with them," Ben said.

Stuart nodded, left.

Bernard arrived ten minutes later. "Aw hell, Ben, that cat kill Airedale."

"No. She was worrying the jaguar when I shot. I killed the dog."

"That cat skin 'bout ruined, Ben."

"I know. I had to use the shotgun."

"Aw, Benny. I hate this, Ben."

"I do too."

"I feed them cats, Ben. I live with them."

"I know."

"I don't like this. No more, Ben, no more."

"Just one more."

Bernard shook his head.

"Listen," Ben said, "I want you to starve the leopard until about eight tomorrow morning, and then give him all the meat he wants."

"Okay."

"Fill him up."

"It slow that cat down, Ben."

"Do it."

"Okay."

"Give him all the red meat he can eat. No water until just before nine o'clock, and then let him drink."

"It slow him down, Ben."

"That leopard's too much for us. If he gets sick when he runs . . ."

"I do it, Ben. But I don't like it."

"You don't like it, huh?"

"No."

Ben lit a cigarette, inhaled, nodded slowly. "I guess you're right. Don't feed the leopard. Give him a little water, not much."

The Indian grinned. "That right, Ben."

"Fuck it."

"Sure, fuck it," Bernard said, grinning.

Eleven

Mrs. Jaramillo was in the kitchen, preparing lunch.

"How did it go, Benny?" she asked.

"Don't ask."

She looked at him.

"Christ, 'Nita, it was awful."

"What happened?"

"The dumb Texas jerks!"

"Shhh, Ben, don't shout."

"They're outside quarreling."

"What happened up there?"

"Chaos."

"You don't want to talk about it?"

"No."

"Okay. Ham-and-cheese sandwiches and gazpacho for lunch. Is that all right?"

"I'm not hungry."

"I can make you something else."

"My stomach is eating itself. I just want a big cold glass of milk."

"We got some buttermilk."

"Great." Ben got a glass from the cupboard, opened the refrigerator, poured the glass full of buttermilk, and carried it over to the table. He sat down, drank half of the milk, wiped his mouth. "We lost a dog, 'Nita."

"Which one?"

"Curly."

"Oh, Ben!"

"I shot him at the same time I shot the jaguar."

"He was a good dog, Benny."

"I know. The cat came down out of the tree and the Airedale moved in to harass her. He was the only one, the other dogs tucked their tails under and scooted. Curly thought he had pals. He didn't."

"Curly was so brave."

"You bet. If the dog had been a coward he'd be alive now. I wish I knew why the things we're told are virtues are so dangerous."

"They wouldn't be virtues if they were easy, Ben."

"Yeah?"

"Virtues are triumphs over our base natures, that's what Father Roybal says."

"Yeah?" Ben grinned at her.

"Did you have to kill the jaguar, Benny?"

"I killed her. The boy went to pieces."

"Did she suffer?"

"A little, not much, not long. 'Nita, the cat looked over and stared at me when we reached her. She looked right at me, she recognized me, and she expected me to help her."

"Oh, Benny!"

"I swear, she expected me to save her from the dogs. She thought I was there to *help* her."

"Please, don't tell me any more."

"Do you remember when I brought her back from Mexico?"

"She was just a baby."

"We kept her in the house until she started tearing up the furniture."

"I fed her with a bottle," Mrs. Jaramillo said. "She could eat solid foods, but she liked milk out of the bottle, too."

"She used to go to sleep on my lap. She weighed sixty-five pounds then, my legs used to go numb."

"Oh, Ben, you killed her."

"What the hell am I doing?" Ben said.

"Ben, this has to stop."

"I know."

"It must stop!"

He nodded.

"You love those animals, Ben, I know you do."

"God, I gave her both barrels, I blew her apart."

"Why are you doing these things?"

"We need the money."

"Sell the leopard. He's a valuable animal. Sell him *alive*!"

"Don't lecture me, 'Nita."

"It's got to stop, Ben."

"I know. After the leopard."

"Now."

"We have to have that sixty-five hundred dollars."

"Benny, please."

He shook his head.

"I've saved money," she said. "I'll give it to you."

"Shut up now," he said. "Goddamn it, 'Nita, the one thing I do not need at this time is another conscience."

"Okay," she said. "All right, Ben."

"This afternoon I'll take them out to see the buffalo. Let's have something special for dinner tonight, with a couple bottles of that good wine. Afterward I'll get them drunk, see if I can't change the mood."

"*Que viva la fiesta,* huh, Benny?"

"*Que viva la fiesta,*" Ben said.

Ben and the entire Stuart family got more or less drunk that night.

Peter Stuart was permitted to have wine with his evening meal. Ben had not seen the boy take more than half a glass, but at dinner that night he drank all of one bottle and started on another. He ate very little; he did not look at anyone; he spoke only in response to a direct question, and then in a sullen mumble; he did not fidget as usual, but was very still. He was still and pale and remote. He just quietly and seriously got drunk and then, without excusing himself, got up from the table and left the room.

"Maybe he's celebrating something," Stuart said.

"Maybe he's very sad," Meredith Stuart said.

Meredith did not normally drink much: a glass of wine with her dinner, and then perhaps a tall bourbon and Coke which lasted until ten o'clock, when she went to bed. She would hold the glass in her hand until the ice melted, lift it to her lips for a tiny sip, run her index finger around the rim, set the glass down on the coffee table, pick it up again, sip. But tonight she drank. Not a great amount, and not sullenly, furiously, like Peter; but enough to alter her behavior. Ben had thought that alcohol would at least partly relieve the tension in the woman, and it did at first: she seemed to soften, become both more relaxed and alert. But after a time she was seized by a different kind of tension. Her movements became jerky. She smoked one cigarette after another. Her eyes, cool and dark, darted here and there, examining the corners of the room, the faces of Ben and her husband, the ceiling, the floor, her hands. She started to tell stories, stopped, laughed, looked away from them. She changed positions in her chair; sat erect, sprawled, hugged herself as if she were very cold. She laughed, shivered, perspired.

Tom Stuart was a drinking man. "I like to drink, Ben," he'd said. "I really do, but I stay on top of it. I'm disciplined. You see me about half drunk every night, but I'm on vacation now, I'm relaxing—but when I'm working, Ben, I seldom take more than two drinks a day. You can believe that."

Ben believed it. The big man drank a lot in the evenings, but it hadn't affected him much until tonight. Stuart liked to tell and listen to stories when he was drinking. He was very attentive while Ben spoke, and then he'd cross his legs, "Yes," tilt back his head, smile, say "Yes, well . . ." and then he would tell a story of his own. He told his stories well, with pace and detail and a droll wit. Stuart was not a humorless man. He was not incapable of laughing at himself. "Ain't that so, Ben? Now, ain't that *so*?" he would say, laughing at the predictable insanity of the human race. He drawled and employed slangy, vulgar grammar when telling his rural barefoot-boy stories; but when he discussed business, or was forced to express a complex thought, his drawl contracted and his syntax was ordered. Like many smart men, Stuart enjoyed appearing stupid. "Just a country boy . . ."

Ben knew that Stuart was complicated and more than a little devious. The barefoot boy with lice in his hair was gone; Stuart was only imitating him. The mules and dogs and grits and catfish and the other dirty-faced, mean-poor kids were gone as well. The nostalgia was a lie, Ben thought. Stuart liked what he had become; despised what he had been.

"Well, Christ, Ben, we were so ignorant bad. And bored? I'll tell you, we'd push a hollow stick up a frog's ass and blow him up. I mean now, blow him up like a balloon." Laughter.

There was considerable self-hatred in his down-home, rock-farmer recollections.

Stuart got drunk and talked a lot that night. He pitied himself and he boasted. He raged. Toward the end, he came close to crying.

Ben learned that Stuart had met and married Meredith after he was well on his way toward becoming rich. That was not surprising. Meredith Stuart had not been the kind of little girl who was permitted to play with boys who had lice in their hair and who blew up frogs with hollow sticks. She'd always worn shoes outdoors, and ribbons in her washed hair, and she had probably learned to play the piano a little, and dance, and curtsy, and say "Oh, please" and "Oh, thank you," and end all of her declarative sentences with a questioning intonation.

It could be, Ben thought, that they had never been able to forgive each other for their backgrounds.

Stuart passed through three distinct phases of drunkenness that night. First he was open, hearty, full of invention and energy; then he became pointlessly hostile, welcoming imaginary offenses; then finally the life seeped out of him, he grew heavy, impossibly heavy and slow, deadened. He dropped his glass, bumped his head against the coffee table while trying to pick it up, cursed his wife for helping him.

Ben and Meredith helped him down the hall and into the bedroom. Stuart protested, struggled, but all his strength was gone. He fell back on the bed. Meredith removed his boots. "Oh, Chris'," Stuart groaned. "Chris', Chris', Chris'." He inhaled deeply, chest swelling, held the breath for a long time, and then slowly exhaled. "Well," he said, and he was asleep.

Ben took the woman's arm and led her through the house to his room. He followed her inside and closed and locked the door behind them. Moonlight silvered the panes of glass overhead, flowed down and broke the room into black-bordered rectangles of light.

"You're going to kill me," she said.

Ben laughed. "No I'm not, honey."

"Kill me," she said.

She was crazy. It was crazy of him to have anything to do with her.

She began undressing. "Kill me, strangle me while we're doing it."

Ben laughed. Why am I laughing? he thought. Get this witch out of here right now. He began to unbutton his shirt.

"You're scary," Ben said, and he laughed. "You are really scary, lady."

Twelve

Ben had hoped to avoid the Stuarts until it was time to go after the leopard, but he overslept and the entire family was sitting around the table when he entered the kitchen.

"Good morning," he said.

Meredith Stuart stared at him coolly, levelly, issuing one of her obscure challenges. She was not smiling, but he could see a latent smile in her eyes and around her mouth. Peter, frowning, watched his mother. Tom Stuart did not turn to acknowledge Ben's greeting.

Mrs. Jaramillo had all four stove burners lighted and was preparing eggs, fried potatoes, bacon, and coffee. Ben inhaled the odors and felt his stomach contract.

He turned away from Meredith's mocking stare. "*Que tal*, 'Nita?" he asked.

"*Que piensas*, Benjamin?" she replied irritably. Then, continuing in Spanish, she said, "I'm making breakfast for the three Texas crazies."

"Careful," Ben said in Spanish. "They might know the language."

The skin around her lips was white with pressure. "They don't. And how did you sleep, Benjamin? Not very good? I heard you talking and tossing in your sleep from one o'clock to three o'clock."

"Jesus," Ben said softly.

"You're a fool, Benny."

" 'Nita, be careful. A lot of these Texans know a little Spanish. The boy probably takes it in school."

"They only know a few words," she said. "They try speaking it to me every now and then."

"I thought you were going to stay at your sister's last night," Ben said.

"We had a fight. I came in through the back door." She dipped the spatula beneath an egg and turned it over. "And you're going hunting with that man," she said. "You put horns on him last night and today you're going up into the mountains with him. He'll be walking behind you all morning with a gun in his hands, Benny." She shook her head and turned two more eggs. "How will that feel?"

"Jesus, 'Nita, what are you trying to do?"

The Stuarts were watching them from the table.

Ben tried to smile at them. "She always chews me out in Spanish," he said.

Bacon fat was sputtering in another frying pan; Mrs. Jaramillo turned down the flame.

"Put some bread in the toaster, will you, Benny?" she said in English.

"Put the goddamned bread in the goddamned toaster yourself," Ben said, and he left the kitchen.

The living room was a stale-smelling mess: beer cans, a whiskey bottle, ashtrays full of crushed cigarette butts, a half-opened can of sardines with the oil congealed, a wedge of cheddar cheese, soda crackers, and pumpernickel bread. Ben hurried through the living room and went out the front door.

There had been another frost last night, though it was less cold now than it had been on the previous mornings. The air felt heavy. There was a smell like rust mingled with the sour odors of sage and wood smoke and adobe soil. The sky was the same incandescent blue, streaked with some wispy bands of cirrus that moved from southwest to northeast. And the atmosphere was slightly hazy; the outlines of the far-off buttes and mountains had lost their sharp edges. A storm coming, Ben thought. But we should have plenty of time to get the cat before it arrives.

He stepped off the porch and lit a cigarette. The smoke tasted bitter and dry. Coffee, you had to have coffee with the first cigarette of the day. His tongue, the inside of his cheeks, and his gums were sore from all the cigarettes he'd smoked last night.

Christ, what was wrong with 'Nita this morning? That was stupid of her; Tom Stuart or the boy might know enough Spanish to understand what she'd been saying. Did Stuart know about last night? No, how could he? The man had been so drunk he could hardly walk and talk. The boy? Well, hell, if 'Nita could hear them last night then the boy could have too. 'Nita's bedroom was way at the rear of the house. But listen, adolescent boys sleep long and deep, they're growing fast, all those glands are going wild and pumping out chemicals, and they burn up a tremendous amount of energy. . . . But maybe the kid couldn't sleep well after his failure with the jaguar. Did Peter know? Would he tell his father? That could prove unpleasant. Tom Stuart had frontier codes that didn't correspond to present-day reality; he wouldn't take kindly to being cuckolded while he slept sixty feet away—he just might blow off Ben's head.

Ben flipped away his cigarette and walked out into the yard. The ground was softening in the sunlight. The frozen puddles were melting now. A soft, almost warm breeze tore dead leaves off the cottonwood trees. It felt more like spring than autumn this morning.

A sentry raven called a warning as Ben approached the cemetery, and then the other ravens cawed and fluttered about in the high branches for a moment before taking off and flying toward the mountains. One of the dogs barked at the ravens, then the others joined in. The hound bitch sounded like a musical instrument, a trombone, or maybe a French horn.

It was still cold in the shadows beneath the trees; the tall yellow weeds and the slanted crosses were coated with a grainy layer of frost. No mounds remained in the cemetery; all of the graves had sunk level to the surrounding ground. He looked at the small stone monuments in the section where his family was buried: his grandfather and grandmother, his grandfather's second wife, 'Nita's aunt, his father, his mother, his sister. There were other stones with Spanish surnames chiseled into them. And more graves, unmarked except for crooked pastel-colored crosses and bouquets of bright plastic flowers. Sometimes, usually in the spring, he saw old women enter the cemetery and replace the old plastic flowers with new ones (he didn't know why, since plastic flowers did not fade or wilt). It was always women who remembered their dead; if there was a male in the groups he was either very young or very, very old. Ben never placed flowers on the graves of his family; he never even cut the weeds. What was the point? He didn't receive any comfort from such little ceremonies; the dead certainly did not.

There was an empty plot next to his sister's grave. It was a hell of a thing, he thought, to know throughout your life where you were going to be buried. A fragment of your mind preceded your body into the hole.

He smoked a cigarette and composed an epitaph for his tombstone.

Creditors, Lawyers, Litigants,
IRS, Ex-Wives, Texans

Here lies Ben,
Beyond your ken.
He ran out of breath,
He ran out of time,
He slipped out of reach.
On this day the ___ of ___, 19___

RIP

Bury me like a dog, Ben, his father had said.
"I did, Pa," Ben said aloud.

Ben remembered that the night after his father had been buried old Bernard had held a private Indian ceremony in the graveyard. It was summer, "cotton" from the cottonwood trees fell like snow, the land seemed to pulse with heat. All the windows of the house had been open, and he had heard Bernard chanting for hours. A fire burned in the cemetery. Later that night Ben had stood on the porch and watched Bernard, a shadow among the fire's lunging shadows, moving around the fire in one of those swaying, bearlike Indian dances. In the morning Ben had found ashes and charred bits of wood on the ground near his father's grave. Neither he nor Bernard had ever mentioned the incident.

And now he recalled his dream of the cats. Yes, it had taken place here, though it had been hot yellow summer in the dream. His corpse had been lying on the other side of the iron fence. He had viewed the scene from where he stood now, yes, by his own future grave. Sprawled, blood-licking cats had been dozing in the shade of these trees, and a hundred more cats had been slowly walking toward him from across the barren ground to the west.

He left the cemetery, crossed the yard, and entered the orchard. Knee-high yellow grass wet with melted frost, dead leaves and rotting fruit on the ground, bare gnarled trees. The branches overhead were a confusing dark tangle, like a child's pencil scribbles, and sharp fragments of sky and wispy cirrus clouds showed through the gaps. Movement caught his eye—a bird, two birds. He moved to an open space, where he could see them clearly. They were hawks, one hundred yards in the air, and they seemed to be fighting: they dived at each other, swerved at the last instant, fell freely for fifty or sixty feet, then separated and climbed, and then once again came together like missiles, but without making contact. Now the hawks separated and flew in opposite directions, describing huge circles in the blue sky, one hawk moving clockwise and the other counterclockwise. They met almost exactly where they had started, closing the two separate circles into a figure eight. They arrived simultaneously at the juncture and had to perform some frantic aerial maneuvers to avoid colliding. They divided again, carved even greater circles in the sky, perfect circles as well as Ben could judge, and as they joined the two circles there was a slight impact, just enough to throw both hawks off balance. They fell a short distance before regaining control. Now the two hawks climbed together, going almost straight up. They broke away then and started new circles. Ben noticed that they alternately flapped their wings and then gilded, flapped and glided, but not in unison. Were they deliberately coordinating their arrival at the starting point? The birds swiftly closed the two circles, and one banked to the left and the other to the right, and then they joined and flew wingtip to wingtip toward the mountains.

Ben watched them until they were just dark specks in the sky. They hadn't been fighting. And he didn't think it had been some kind of three-dimensional mating dance—this was autumn, not spring. Were they simply playing, then? Hawks? Why not, he thought, hell, why not? The hawks had made him feel good—good enough, anyway, to face the Stuarts for another day.

They had finished breakfast and were sitting around the table drinking coffee and smoking.

"Where's 'Nita?" Ben asked. "I'm hungry."

"Don't know," Stuart said. "She left a few minutes ago."

"I just saw the damnedest aerobatic display," Ben said. He got a cup and saucer from the cupboard and poured some coffee. "Two hawks. I wish you could have seen them. They were playing together, I think. Just out-and-out no-account, time-wasting frivolity."

Ben carried his coffee over to the table and sat down. Meredith Stuart was directly across from him: a mistake, he should have taken the other empty chair. Her chin was tilted up, her eyes were half-lidded. She was not mocking or challenging him now. She had retreated far back into herself, apparently staring at him only because he had interrupted her view of the wall. Peter sat next to his mother. Tom Stuart was by the window.

"I've seen a lot of hawks," Ben said, "but I've never seen anything like that."

"Wished I'd of seen it," Stuart said quietly, without interest. He looked very fat, hunched over as he was; he had a big frame and he could carry the excess weight gracefully enough while erect, but when he was relaxed he appeared grossly out of condition. His face was pale and puffy this morning, his eyes small, and when he removed the spoon from his coffee and placed it in the saucer Ben could see that his hand was trembling.

"Are you going to be able to shoot with that hang-over of yours?" Ben asked.

"I'll be fine." His voice, always low and phlegmy, now had a raw hoarse note in it.

"I guess we did some drinking last night," Ben said.

"We did that."

"I don't feel too bad, considering." Ben sipped his coffee and then slowly lowered his cup to the saucer. His hand was steady, without a tremor. He did not look at Meredith, though he was very much aware of her presence, her stare. He thought of how she had looked last night, unclothed, and how there had been something demented in the intensity of her sexual heat. He wished he could spend one week with her, just seven days locked in a small room, turn his lust free, cut loose all the restraints and inhibitions, use both himself and her up. And then just forget about sex for the rest of his life.

"What?" Ben said.

Stuart: "I said, it must be about time to go."

Ben glanced at his watch. "It's getting there."

"Mere, Peter, why don't you two get ready now."

"I'm not going this morning," she said.

"What?"

"No," she said. "You men go off without me today."

"Mere, stop this crap and get ready."

"Peter is staying here," she said. "His asthma is very bad again. I'll stay with him."

"Peter?" Stuart said.

The boy shifted uneasily. He raised one of his hands from below the table, folded it into a fist, and forced a cough into it. He did not look at his father. "I don't feel well," he said.

"You sound all right to me."

"I'm sick."

"Jesus Christ."

"Tom, you don't want us along anyway," Meredith said sweetly. "We'll just be in the way."

"Get ready. Both of you."

"Father," Peter said, "I almost choked to death yesterday."

"It wasn't that bad."

"If it wasn't for the Adrenalin I might have died." His voice was querulous now, and accusing.

"Bullshit," Stuart said.

"Anyway, Father"—smug now, vindictively happy—"yesterday you said you'd quit on me."

"Meredith?" Stuart said.

"I'm going to stay here with Peter."

"I want you to be with me, Meredith."

She slowly shook her head, smiling at him. "Oh, Tom, we all know how huge and competent you are in the outdoors," she said in that lilting, whispery voice. "We don't have to watch you, darling, we know. Just bring the leopard home to us and tell us all about it."

Stuart was baffled. He looked at his wife and son, then at Ben.

"Just as well, really," Ben said. "That leopard is likely to run us all over those hills."

Stuart abruptly got up and walked out of the kitchen.

"He really does want us to see him in action," Meredith Stuart said. "He wants to show off. Tom is like a boy in so many ways. All men are—you never completely grow up."

Ben shrugged.

"I just want to stay here and relax. I want to go back to bed, stretch like one of those cats, yawn, turn over, and sleep again."

Peter watched his mother.

"And then I want to get up and go to the refrigerator and get a pear, bite into it, and let the sticky juice run down my chin."

Ben sipped his coffee; it was cold. He lit a cigarette.

"And maybe I'll take a hot, hot bath with scents and oils and steam." Her eyes were dilated. When she smiled Ben saw that her teeth were locked together.

"And then dry myself off with a coarse towel, rub my skin red, and then maybe go back to sleep again."

"It sounds like a boring day," Ben said.

"Oh, but it won't be."

Peter slowly arose from his chair. "My mother is a whore," he said, and then he left the room.

Meredith leaned toward Ben. "What did Peter say?"

"He said you were a whore."

She smiled.

"He knows about last night?" Ben asked.

She nodded. "I told him."

"You told him! Why, for Christ's sake?"

"He asked me."

"My God!"

"I never lie to Peter."

"Does your husband know about last night?"

"I don't know."

"Do you care if he finds out?"

She slowly shook her head.

"Maybe Peter's gone to tell him."

"Maybe."

"And maybe Tom will kill me. A hunting accident."

"Maybe," she said, and she smiled again.

Ben got up and started for the doorway.

"Wait." She got up, moved away from the table, and backed up against the wall. She tilted her head back and closed her eyes. "Come over and touch me here. And here."

"You're crazy," Ben said. "And you're trying to get me killed." Ben went to his room, got the shotgun and half a dozen cartridges, and went outside.

He loaded the dogs into the camper shell of the pickup, started the engine, drove the truck around, and parked it by the porch steps. He turned on the radio: an advertisement for jock itch; the sports news; another advertisement, this one a woman talking narcissistically about "my gas" and the remedy for "my gas," though it sounded as though she'd be bereft without her gas; an agriculture report . . . Ben turned off the radio.

Oh, that weird, murderous bitch.

Stuart came out of the house. He was wearing the .357 Magnum revolver in the belt holster and carrying a fiberglass hunting bow and a quiver of arrows.

Ben got out of the truck. "No," he said.

"Ben," Stuart said softly, "don't fuck with me today."

"Get your rifle."

"I'm using this," he said, raising the bow.

"No you're not."

"Men say yes to me when I want them to, Ben."

"Not me."

"Ben, I'll show you how I get men to say yes."

Stuart opened the truck door and placed his bow and quiver on the seat. He turned, reached into his breast pocket, withdrew two slips of paper, unfolded them, and gave them to Ben. They were checks: one for the other half of the money owed on the three cats, $6,750, and the other a check for $2,500. The smaller check had "bonus" scrawled at the bottom.

"Now let's go, Ben."

Ben wanted to tell Stuart to take the check and shove it. But he didn't. He started to speak, hesitated, then folded the two checks and put them into his wallet. He felt a little sick. Then he closed off a part of his mind; he would deal with the implications of this act later.

"Yes," Ben said.

He drove up through the desert and parked the truck among the piñons. They got out. The sky was still streaked with furry cirrus clouds. Shadows of the clouds lay across the blue-hazed desert in long slanting bars. The clouds were very high, well above the mountain peaks. It was warm now. One hundred yards away two magpies quarreled over a piece of carrion.

"Another fine day," Stuart said. He was calm now, relaxed after finally having won his dollar-victory.

I can always tear up this check, Ben thought. After the leopard is dead I can walk up to Stuart and rip this check to pieces under his big nose.

"We're going to get a storm," Ben said.

"When?"

"This evening, tonight."

Stuart studied the sky. "Those clouds don't look like they contain anything."

"Those aren't the clouds that'll drop on us."

"What time is it now, Ben?"

"A quarter to nine."

"Fifteen minutes more." Stuart slowly inhaled and then exhaled.

"Nervous?" Ben asked.

"Not nervous, but a little high. Like the high you get before the start of a big football game. That's always a good sign, that up. You have to have it to function at the max."

The dogs were whining and scratching around inside the camper shell.

"Listen," Ben said. "Can you use that bow?"

Stuart nodded.

"Because that leopard—"

"Leopards aren't big cats."

"This one is a big leopard."

"I mean, I've shot a five-hundred-pound lion and a four-hundred-and-fifty-pound lion."

"I've studied this leopard. And I've done some reading on them. They're stealthy. They're fast, so goddamned fast. And strong—a leopard can bite through the neck into the spine of a good-sized antelope, throw it over his back, carry it for a mile, and then run up a tall tree with it."

"I know. In Africa I had a leopard on my license, but I never got one. We'd sit in a blind for hours. There'd be some rotting meat up in the fork of the tree. We had to remain absolutely still for hours. A leopard appeared once at dusk. There was nothing, and then by Christ there was a leopard standing at the base of the tree. I raised my rifle, but I must have made a sound, or the cat sensed something, because then it was gone, Ben. It was in my sights and then it vanished. I never saw another one."

"You'll see this one," Ben said. "But if you miss or just wound that cat with your arrow, I'm going to let go with my shotgun."

"I won't miss." Stuart seemed sleepy, drunk.

A cloud blotted out the sun for a moment; they were immersed in cool shadow, and then the sun emerged and the light returned as if a rheostat were gradually being turned up.

"What time is it now?"

"Ten to."

Stuart was silent for a time, seeming to doze in the sunlight, and then he said: "My wife has been in and out of institutions for the past seven years."

Ben looked at him.

Stuart shifted lazily, said: "She was released from the last one five weeks ago."

Ben cleared his throat.

"She has been diagnosed as schizophrenic."

"I'm sorry, Ben said.

"I brought her here, to the country, for a rest."

"I don't see how this—the killing—would do her any good."

"The prognosis isn't good for schizophrenia. They've tried just about everything with Meredith, psychoanalysis, electroshock, chemotherapy—name it. She seems to get well for a while and then she goes back. I guess she'll spend the rest of her life in and out of institutions."

"Shit," Ben said. "I'm sorry."

"Meredith is a beautiful woman, and she's highly sexed. Sex is a part of her sickness, a symptom, I guess. There are no controls, Ben, nothing to hold her back. She'll go off with anyone, anytime. You know? The lady is sick. One of the psychiatrists at the last institution was fucking her regularly. He's been discharged and his license will be pulled. But, Ben, what kind of cold son of a bitch would take that kind of advantage of a sick woman?"

Ben did not reply.

"You know, Ben, it's been hard for me and Peter. But we love her. Lord God, we do love her. And it makes me sick to think of a man using her like she was some kind of masturbation machine. It just sickens me. I don't understand it at all. What kind of man would take her off and fuck her raw, knowing that the lady is ill? What do you think, Ben? Just what do you think about that?"

"I don't know what to tell you," Ben said.

"Well, it must be about nine o'clock."

"Three minutes to go."

"I guess Meredith will have to go back again."

"Look, Stuart, I want to—"

"Stay to my left when I'm drawing on the leopard," Stuart said. "You'll be in my field of vision and distract me if you're on my right side."

"Okay," Ben said.

"Listen to the dogs scrambling around in there. The Indian must have blown his whistle a little early."

"Christ, Stuart, I don't know what to tell you."

"Have you checked your shotgun, Ben? You

wouldn't want to pull the triggers on empty chambers, if it comes down to that."

The dogs were yelping and scratching and throwing their bodies against the walls of the camper. Ben walked around to the back and opened the doors. The dogs tumbled out one atop another, smelling of dog and urine and shit—they simply could not control their bladders and bowels when they heard the whistle. They jumped up on Ben and Stuart, whimpered, ran around in diminishing circles, squirted urine. The hound greeted them briefly and then loped off into the trees. The other dogs milled about in confusion, and then one peeled off and followed the hound, and then the others fell into ranks, yelping and barking, and began the chase.

Thirteen

*B*en started jogging through the trees. He could
hear Stuart's heavy breathing and the thud of his
footfalls behind. After a few minutes there were
fewer piñons and more pine and spruce. The soil
gradually lost its reddish hue. The dogs were far
ahead and a little to the north now; he could hear the
clear two-note baying of the hound and the barking
of the others. It was a warm, more than usually hu-
mid day, and he had already sweated through his
light wool shirt. The shotgun was heavy.

He ran until he started to get an ache in his side,
and then he stopped and turned. Stuart, having a hard
time of it, came trotting heavily in and out of the
trees. His face was red and shiny with sweat. There
were big sweat patches beneath his armpits and in the

crotch of his trousers. He stopped, breathing hard, his chest swelling.

"Shit, Ben," he said. "How do you expect"—he inhaled deeply, slowly exhaled, forcing the air out against the pressure of his lips—"me to shoot if my"—another break—"heart is jumping around and I'm all shaky from running?"

"We'll jog for a while, walk, jog again, walk some more. We'll rest you for the shot."

Stuart bent over, shook his head.

"Listen," Ben said. He waited. "Hear? The dogs are already a long way off. That leopard's taking them for a run. He'll tree soon. We can't let him rest too long or he'll drop down out of the tree and kill about three dogs and then take off again. Come on."

He turned and started walking swiftly up a steep hill. There was a lot of brushy undergrowth. He held the shotgun over his shoulder now, muzzle forward and down. The trees were taller and broader at the base, and the sunlight gave the upper branches a greenish-gold tint. Here and there the shafts of sunlight filtered to the loamy forest floor, settling in dappled amebalike blurs which expanded and contracted as the wind moved the tree branches. Ben climbed to the top of the hill.

"Ho, Ben."

He looked up. Bernard was sitting on a spruce branch twenty feet off the ground. He held his old single-shot twenty-gauge by the barrel with his left hand and hugged the tree trunk with his right. He grinned down at them.

"What the hell are you doing up that tree?"

"I'm a-scared of that cat, Benny," Bernard said. "Listen to dogs. That cat coming back."

Ben listened. The dogs did sound closer now. "The leopard's circling back?" he asked.

"Think so."

"Leopards climb trees, Bernard. What if the dogs chase him up your tree?"

"I shit out of luck," he said, squinting his eyes and grinning.

The sound of the dogs continued to approach, and then suddenly there was a new note in their barking and howling.

"He in tree now, Ben," Bernard said.

Ben started trotting off toward the dogs. Stuart followed. They went down into a shallow depression and then climbed a long, steep incline to a ridge. The dogs were close now. Ben stopped and waited for Stuart.

"Not far from here," Ben said.

Stuart nodded, reached over his shoulder, and withdrew an arrow. It had an aluminum shaft, plastic vanes, and a razor-edged steel arrowhead. Stuart was breathing deeply; there was a hoarse whistling in his throat. His face was crimson, lumpy-looking, and Ben could see a thick blue-green vein pulsing in the center of his forehead.

"You okay?"

Stuart nodded again.

"Catch your breath. The leopard should stay treed for a while yet."

Stuart did not reply.

"Sweat out your hangover yet, Tom?"

"Fuck you, Ben."

Ben turned away so that Stuart would not see his grin. He felt pretty good now, though winded and leg-tired: Stuart was not going to kill him, the dogs had treed the leopard, and in a minute or two there was going to be excitement, maybe even great danger. The excitement made him feel hollow inside, and jumpy, and very light, as if gravity had been reduced by half. Stuart would surely miss his arrow shot or just wound the leopard, and then it would drop stiff-legged and snarling out of the tree. It would be close. Maybe it would charge. Leopards were fast, so fast—was there anything so spring-tightened all-out cata-pulting fast as a cat? And Ben would kill it. He did not want to kill that animal, and yet he very much wanted to kill it. He was glad he had the shotgun; he didn't think he was cool enough, or a good enough shot, to stop a charging leopard with a rifle.

"Okay," Ben said. "Move slow when we get near the leopard. He'll be occupied with the dogs. I'll cover you while you make your shot."

Stuart was breathing more normally now. "Just don't shoot, Ben. That's my cat."

"If you miss, he's mine."

"I won't miss."

They started up the easy slope of the ridge. There seemed to be a panicky note in the barking of the dogs; they sensed that this was no ordinary cat, not a mountain lion, not a jaguar. Maybe they could smell the difference, Ben thought.

After about sixty yards Ben broke through the brush into a small clearing. He stopped. Stuart moved up on his left side. Ben could smell Stuart: a kind of sour-milk scent, aftershave, his metallic breath—was his own sense of smell more acute now?

The leopard lay flat on a thick branch of a white, leafless and barkless oak tree. Ben knew that tree. He had collected honey from it when he was a boy, and years afterward it had been struck by lightning. It had been dead for several years now, but it remained standing, rotten, worm-grooved, looking as if it had been sculpted out of solid bone. The crooked white branches stood out against the deep blue of the sky. The smaller branches and twigs clattered dryly in the wind.

The leopard was tired; his sides heaved convulsively. His jaws were open, and Ben could see the pink tongue and a gleam of teeth. Sunlight ignited the cat's fur and made it blaze with a fierce, alien yellow light. The dogs cautiously approached the tree, stopped with their front legs braced at an angle and their haunches low, then slowly backed up, barking furiously. One of the dogs saw Ben and grew bold; it wagged its tail briefly, moved in beneath the branch and leaped vertically, fell back, leaped again. The leopard calmly watched.

"A little closer," Stuart whispered. He had nocked an arrow into the bowstring.

They slowly moved out into the clearing.

The dogs were encouraged by their presence: they snarled, barked, leaped toward the cat.

"Okay," Stuart said.

They were forty feet away from the tree.

Ben thumbed back the hammers on his shotgun. The clicks attracted the leopard's attention, and he turned toward them. Ben had difficulty focusing his eyes on the cat; his coal-black rosettes seemed to jump out and then recede in opposition to the pale gold of the fur. The wind rose, ruffled the fur and showed a paler yellow, almost a white. The cat slowly rose to his feet. He watched them. His eyes were a cold speckled amber.

Stuart slowly raised his bow. The cat watched, hunching his back slightly, flicking his tail.

"Oh, shit, man," Ben said. "Do it." Or maybe he hadn't said it; maybe he'd only thought the words.

Stuart had the bow fully drawn now.

The leopard was beautiful, terrible. His cold cold defiance triggered contradictory emotions in Ben: he wanted to laugh, and to vomit.

The bowstring twanged, and the arrow shaft, as thin and straight as a beam of light, connected origin and goal, time and space, and pierced the leopard's heart.

No! The arrow, a continuous white line against the sky, had been flying so true that Ben had felt a surge of near-affection for Stuart—a reliable man—but then, my God, the cat had reflexively flicked out a forepaw and deflected the arrow. It went into his hind leg, and the cat coiled with a hissing scream, turned, and cleanly bit off the arrow shaft.

Ben fired. He was too slow. The tree limb burst, spraying pieces of white wood, but by then the cat was dropping down among the dogs. A yellow-and-black blur, and a dog came tumbling end over end across the ground. A yelp, another spinning dog. Ben fired again.

Too late; you had to anticipate this cat, guess his movements and then lead him as you'd lead a flying bird. And then the leopard was gone, using the fringe of brush and trees, even the light, in a magical way. The cat was there, screaming and swatting dogs, and then he was simply gone. Twice Ben caught a flash of mottled light moving across the forest floor, but he was not sure that it was the leopard, and anyway, his shotgun was empty.

The hound, baying, went off after the leopard. The remaining dogs gathered around Ben and Stuart, whining, trying to lick their hands. One of them had been raked from shoulder to tail, and its skin hung down in bloody strips. It looked as if an artery had been severed. Another dog, eviscerated, lay panting in the dust. Its intestines had spilled out in slick grayish-pink coils, and the animal lifted his head to lick them, then fell back. Ben borrowed Stuart's revolver and shot the two wounded dogs.

"I'm sorry."

"It was a pretty good shot."

"No, it was too far back."

"The cat deflected the arrow, Stuart."

"I didn't see that."

"He did. Can you imagine the eye and reflexes and speed it would take to do that? Jesus. He plucked that arrow right out of the air."

"He couldn't have deflected a bullet."

"That's right," Ben said.

"I'm sorry. You were right."

"Oh, Stuart, listen, man, we're in deep trouble now." Ben was happy. He didn't know why; he knew that actually he should be the most miserable man in three states, but he wasn't, he felt unaccountably exhilarated.

The hound came out of the brush with her head down, hindquarters low, tail whipping.

"She was scared to follow the cat alone," Stuart said.

"Of course she was. She can smell the guts of her comrades. Well, I don't know, Stuart. Jesus. A wounded leopard." Ben felt a grin stretching his mouth. He really shouldn't be grinning now.

"What can we do?"

"I don't know. Christ. It's bad, really bad," Ben said, grinning.

"Ben, just what the hell do you want to do?"

"Well, I don't know. Maybe we ought to go back to the house and wait there for a few hours. Let the cat bleed and stiffen up. Damn, Stuart, did you see that cat?"

"I saw him."

"Yes, I believe we'd better let that cat alone for a few hours to bleed and stiffen and get sick."

"I'll get my rifle."

"That's a fair idea," Ben said.

They met Bernard on the way down. Ben told him what had happened and what their plans were.

"Do you want to come down to the house with us?"

"I don't stay *here*, Ben."

Fourteen

Back down on the desert Ben saw two tarantulas within one hundred yards. It was going to rain; the spiders moved to higher ground to avoid being drowned in their burrows.

Peter met them at the door. "Is he dead?"

His father brushed by him.

"Wounded," Ben said. "We've got to get back up there." He passed into the living room, Bernard following, and then Peter closed the door.

"Is it going to be all right?" Peter asked.

"Sure." Ben walked to the kitchen. "One more for lunch," he told Mrs. Jaramillo. "Bernard came down with us."

"The same number for lunch, Ben. The lady went into town. She said she wouldn't be back until two or three this afternoon."

"Okay."

"Soup and spaghetti and meatballs for lunch, Ben."

"That's fine," he said, although he thought that was a little heavy considering all the hiking they would have to do that afternoon.

"The leopard, Ben?"

"Wounded. We have to go back up there."

He returned to the living room. Tom Stuart sat on the couch with his legs sprawled full length on the floor. He looked tired. If you think you're tired now, Ben thought, wait until this evening. Bernard was sitting in the high-backed wooden chair by the south wall; his feet did not quite touch the floor. Peter stood near the television.

"How about a beer?" Ben asked.

"Sure. Sounds good," Stuart said.

"I'll get it," Peter said, starting for the kitchen.

"Wait. Bernard, want a beer?" Ben figured that one can of beer would not push the old man off the wagon.

"No beer, Ben."

"Two then," Ben said. "And one for yourself if you want it, Peter."

The boy went into the kitchen.

"Damn!" Stuart said. "Damn, damn, damn! I still don't know how I missed the cat at that range."

"I told you, you didn't miss him, he deflected the arrow with his paw."

"I hardly believe that's possible."

"I saw the hardly possible, then."

"That arrow had to be going over one hundred miles an hour. Well over."

"Men can hit the stuffing out of a baseball that's

going over one hundred miles per hour with a narrow bat," Ben said. "And I don't believe the man's been born yet with reflexes quicker than a leopard."

"Yeah, but, Ben, a batter is waiting for the ball, expecting it."

"The leopard saw the arrow coming toward him. Didn't know what it was, flicked out a paw."

Peter returned with three cans of Coors. He handed one to his father, one to Ben, and kept the third.

"Mrs. Jaramillo told me that lunch wouldn't be long," Peter said.

"That leopard's got to be bad hurt," Stuart said.

"I don't know. The arrow got him in the flank."

"And it didn't pass through, Ben?"

"No. It looked like it entered at an angle, because of the deflection. He bit off the shaft."

"The arrowhead must have hit bone, then. It might have fractured the bone."

"Maybe."

"And the arrowhead is still in there, chewing up muscle and ligament."

Ben nodded.

"It might work around and cut a big artery or a tendon."

"Yeah, well, we can't count on him dying on his own. Not with that wound. Cats are tough. I had a house cat that the dogs caught. That cat had been chewed and shaken and bitten and torn every which way. It was just a rag when I saw it. Guts hanging out, head nearly off—but it was still breathing. And it took two head shots from my .22 rifle before it finally quit. Don't count on your flank shot slowing down the big cat too much."

Peter was watching them. Bernard was now dozing in the big chair, snoring softly.

"I'm not an *expert* archer," Stuart said. "But I can shoot."

Ben sipped his beer.

"That leopard'll be five counties away by the time we get back up there."

"No, he's hurt all right. Not fatally hurt by any means, but hurt. He'll lay up somewhere to heal."

"Well, I suppose we got to hunt him down."

"Christ, yes! I don't like to think about what would happen if some hiker or hunter wandered into that animal."

"Is he very dangerous?" Peter said.

"Very," Ben said.

"Now, Ben," Stuart said. "Sure the leopard is dangerous, but he's not going to eat anybody up."

"Listen, that cat is hurt. He knows who hurt him. We did—men did. He isn't going to feel kindly toward our species. Do you think he doesn't know that *we're* dangerous to him? What is he going to do the next time he smells man? Run away? Maybe. Maybe. But cats don't lack confidence, that cat especially. He's smart, that leopard. He's fierce. I know him. I think he's going to try to kill any human who comes near him."

"Ben, it's possible, but I don't expect it."

"Expect it, please."

"They're considered vermin in Africa."

"Sure, and those vermin—not even hurt—will carry off and eat human beings."

"Jesus," Peter said quietly. He watched them.

"And the reason in Africa you *have to* track down

and kill wounded vermin like leopards and lions is because they're likely to eviscerate the first man, woman, or child they can find."

Stuart was grinning now. "Okay, Ben. Okay."

"It may be your ass," Ben said. "It isn't going to be mine."

Stuart, still grinning, looked at Peter. "Where's your mother?"

"She went into town."

"What for?"

"I don't know. I guess she wanted to see the galleries."

"Where's my rifle?"

"In the room," Peter said. "My room."

"Get it for me."

Peter set his beer down on the television and started down the hall.

"Did you clean my rifle, Peter?"

The boy stopped, turned. "I forgot."

"You forgot."

"I meant to . . ."

"Weren't you supposed to clean it after using it, Peter?"

"Yes, sir." The boy's eyes flicked between his father and Ben.

"Haven't I told you that you *always* clean a weapon as soon as you can after firing it?"

"Yes, sir. But I was . . . you see . . . I hated it. I didn't want to touch it."

Stuart closed his eyes for a time, opened them.

"I'm sorry," Peter said.

"You're sorry."

"Hell," Ben said. "What's the need for this? That

barrel isn't going to pit in one day, not in this climate."

"This doesn't concern you, Ben."

"I'll clean the rifle now," Peter said.

"You won't forget, will you, Peter?"

"No, sir."

"I've showed you how to disassemble and clean a rifle, haven't I, Peter?"

The boy nodded. He glanced at Ben, at the sleeping Indian, back at his father. He clenched and unclenched his hands.

"Do you think you can remember how to do it?"

Peter started to speak, but could only nod.

"Will you run a clean rag through the barrel afterwards, to get rid of the excess oil? So the firearm will shoot true?"

"Please," Peter said.

"Please? Please what, Peter?"

The boy tried to smile and failed.

"Please what, Peter?"

Peter shook his head.

"Peter?"

The boy closed his eyes.

"You said the word 'please,' Peter. Please what?"

The boy started sobbing. "Please . . . please don't . . . don't . . . humiliate me anymore."

"Go and clean my rifle now, Peter."

The boy opened his eyes, turned, and went down the hallway.

"You son of a bitch," Ben said softly.

Stuart looked at him. "I'll forget you said that, Ben."

Ben nodded. "What counts to me is that I remember that I said it."

Peter stayed in his room during lunch. Ben got up from the table first. "I'll pack a couple of rucksacks with food and a tarp and all. If we don't kill that cat before dark we may have to bivouac up there tonight."

Stuart shrugged.

" 'Nita, tell Mrs. Stuart that we just may not be down until tomorrow."

"All right, Benny."

"You going to take them shit-eating dogs, Ben?" Stuart asked.

"Just the hound."

Before leaving the house, Stuart examined his rifle. He removed the bolt, set it aside, put a small patch of white paper in the breech, tilted the rifle back, and looked down the barrel. "Okay," he said, nodding. Then he replaced the bolt, loaded the clip and slipped it home, and levered a round into the chamber.

"You did fine, Peter," he said.

"I've always tried to please you," Peter said bitterly. "Don't you know that?"

"Why no," Stuart said. "No, I don't believe I do know that."

Fifteen

*I*t took them an hour to hike up to the clearing beneath the lightning-struck oak. When they emerged from the fringe of woods a flock of ravens scattered, cawing, explosively beating their wings, rising and flapping away to perch in the high branches of a pine. The ravens had eaten the eyes of the two dogs, mutilated their tongues, and dragged entrails over the ground.

"Them birds didn't waste time," Stuart said.

The hound, sniffing the air and whining, pulled at the leash; Ben restrained her.

"Maybe we ought to bury the dogs," Stuart said.

"We haven't got the time," Ben said.

Ben dragged the hound across the clearing until she was distracted by the scent of the leopard.

"What do you think, Bernard?"

"I don't like to go first, Ben."

"You don't have to go first. You don't have to track, we've got the dog for that."

"You go first with dog. I go in middle, okay? This man"—meaning Stuart—"he come behind."

Ben nodded. "That's how I figured it."

"Watch out," Bernard told Stuart. "That cat maybe come up back us. Keep wind in his face. Watch out."

The hound led them over a series of ever-bigger hills and then along a narrow ravine to a creek. The cat had paused here to drink; they could see its footprints in the mud, and little starbursts of blood scattered here and there. After drinking the cat had gone directly up the old game trail toward high country.

The path rose steeply through the trees, crossing and recrossing the creek many times. The sound of the water changed: sometimes there was a crashing roar that echoed off the hills on either side, and other times there was no more than a soft humming, a liquid buzz. The creek was shallow and clear and fast, pouring whitely over the falls and mushrooming around boulders and half-sunken logs. The trees that had fallen over past seasons were all unnaturally white, without bark or branches or living grace. They lay askew, slanting down the hillsides, caught at angles by standing trees, bridging the creek. Intricate worm channels had been carved into the white wood. Some of them had been splintered by bears. Trees had fallen into the creek and formed small dams behind which the water was deep and still. In those pools the light made bright rings on the pebbled bottom and water spiders cast trembling shadows. Trout arrowed across the pools and vanished beneath a bank.

They moved very quietly upwind and so surprised some animals: three doe mule deer that stared near-sightedly at them and then bounded stiff-legged up an embankment; a cock turkey; half a dozen blue grouse, nearly as tame as barnyard chickens; and a young bear that squealed like a pig as it hurtled noisily through the brush. Ben heard the bear before he saw it, and he felt his heart jump and then hesitate, and he was momentarily paralyzed. He could not react and do the things he had told himself to do: release the dog, simultaneously raise the shotgun and cock the hammers, aim, fire. He had stood there, frozen. Then he saw that it was only a bear. He knew that he would have been a dead man if it had been the leopard.

For the first time in years Ben felt physical fear: his mouth dried, the hair on his neck and forearms bristled, his insides contracted, and he felt a sudden need to urinate. Before he had been alert, quietly exhilarated, the hunter. It seemed an uneven contest, three armed men against a cat, but still he was afraid. His fear was sickening and unlike any fear he'd previously experienced; it was old and rotten, was related to panic, and he could smell it on himself.

"Christ," Stuart said. "For an instant I thought that was the cat."

"So did I," Ben said. "But the leopard will come silently if he comes."

"Were you in the Army?" Stuart asked.

"Yes."

"Ever in combat?"

"No."

"I wonder if this is what it's like."

"Not now, Stuart. No more talking. We've got to concentrate."

They climbed higher, and now there were tall aspens scattered among the pine and spruce and fir trees; their white, birchlike trunks rose straight and branchless for fifty or sixty feet and then burst into bright gold leaves that spun and buzzed in the wind. The sky was completely covered with nimbostratus clouds. They had gained about two thousand feet of altitude in three hours and were close to ten thousand feet. Stuart was having a hard time of it: he breathed rapidly, and twice he slipped and almost fell.

Ben stopped. "Let's rest for a few minutes," he said.

"Going to rain, Ben," Bernard said.

"I know."

"Dog maybe lose smell."

"Then you'll have to track the leopard. It looks like the cat is going high, Bernard."

The Indian nodded. "Sure. Cat hurt, go fast and high."

Ben realized that none of them looked at the others while they talked; instead they continually scanned the surrounding terrain, peering into the brush and trees, weapons ready. He did not know if Stuart and Bernard felt the strain as acutely as he did; their faces were impassive. Ben believed that his face was impassive too, though he could feel a muscular tic pulling at the corner of his mouth. He could feel it, but he did not think they would be able to see it.

They went on. After half an hour it began to rain lightly. Rain accentuated the odors of resin and rot. The sky was dark with shapeless clouds. It was cold now, and they had to pause to put on their jackets. Bernard wore an old plaid wool coat and arranged his blanket so that it formed a hooded thigh-length robe.

They went on. The creek cut straight through a grassy meadow, entered the woods again, and then arced around a squarish solid-granite block that was as big as a hotel. A wooded hill rose to their right. Above the trees to their left, a mile or two away, they could see a long line of steep, thousand-foot-high cliffs. Cloud misted the upper level. Ben had climbed on those cliffs when he was a boy. It was rugged country, thickly forested on the valley floor, rising to smooth granite slabs that looked as if molten stone had flowed downhill before finally solidifying, and then the vertical walls began, broken here and there by caves, narrow ledges, chimneys, and sawtooth pinnacles. Rough terrain, a natural refuge for the wounded leopard; but the hound continued to lead them up the trail alongside the creek.

The ground steepened and the creek came down the hillside in a series of two- and three-foot-high waterfalls. The air was misty here. The creek crashed and throbbed, and there was a clicking sound of stones being rolled along the bed. The wind gusted, blew the rain into their faces. The slope decreased, and they entered a large grove of aspens.

"Ben," Stuart called. "Can we rest a minute?"

Ben stopped and turned. Bernard was right behind him, almost on his heels, but Stuart had fallen thirty feet behind.

"Try to stay with us," Ben said.

Stuart joined them, his face red and swollen-looking, his breath smoking in the cold air.

"Jesus," he said.

Ben smiled. "Tired?"

"I didn't know I was in this bad a shape."

"We're close to eleven thousand feet here."

"Is that it? The altitude?"

"That and the fact of your sorry physical condition."

Stuart smiled thinly, nodded. "Do you think the dog knows what she's doing? She's sniffing at the ground all right, and pulling on the leash, but I got an idea that shit eater is just taking us for a walk."

"She's got a good nose," Ben said.

"Okay, but this rain . . ."

"She's got the scent all right."

"I haven't seen any blood for a long time."

Ben turned to Bernard. "Have you seen any track?" he asked.

"No, Ben. Rain wash away, probably."

"Well, the dog's got something."

"Cat no around here," Bernard said.

"How do you know?"

"I know."

"Don't give me any of that noble-savage-in-tune-with-nature crap, Bernard," Ben said.

Bernard grinned, showing his crooked yellow teeth.

Stuart turned and looked intently into the brush for a moment, then relaxed. "Is this still Forest Service land?"

"Yes."

"Indian land," Bernard said.

"This land is administered by the Forest Service," Ben said.

"Indian land."

"It used to be Indian land, but it isn't anymore."

"We get it back."

"You probably will," Ben said.

"Get it all back, Ben." The Indian grinned. "All of it. Kick your ass out of here. All your ass. Fuck you, Ben. We skin you like rabbit. Put you on anthill. Honey in your eyes."

"Don't give me any of that Warner Brothers stuff, Bernard."

"Bend two trees like this. Tie one tree to one leg, other tree to other leg. Let go the tree. Oh-oh, two Ben now. Left Ben and right Ben." His face crinkled in a huge grin, and his eyes almost vanished in the network of wrinkles.

"Bernard loves Western movies," Ben told Stuart. "The old ones, where the Indians lost."

The old man grinned. "Give you to squaws," he said. "They cut you to pieces, feed dogs. Dogs shit you. We bury."

"Look how cheerful he is," Ben said. "He must be right, that leopard's probably in Colorado by now."

"You know," Stuart said, "I have the feeling that the leopard's not around here, too."

"So do I," Ben said. "That means we're all getting careless. Let's get going, and concentrate."

The creek curved through the grove of trees and entered a level clearing about fifty yards long and thirty yards wide. Bare white tree trunks, looking like the fallen marble columns of a ruin, were scattered around the open space. The grass had turned brown, but there were still a few tenacious autumn flowers growing along the banks of the creek.

They passed through the clearing and entered the forest. The dog was having more and more difficulty keeping the scent; she lost it, circled, nose to the ground, picked it up and followed it for a short distance, lost it again. It was cold in the wind and rain; their clothes were soaked through, they exhaled big clouds of vapor. The dog's wet fur steamed in the cold, and she shivered miserably whenever they paused.

She completely lost the scent at the source of the creek. They were in an amphitheater of high mountains. The timberline was only a few hundred feet higher. Most of the trees were bare on the windward side. It was fairly level where they stood, but the ground gradually sloped upward on three sides until reaching the timberline, and then steepened and rose up to ridges that approached thirteen thousand feet. Ben could glimpse the bare, dun-colored ridges through the roof of trees. They went on farther, and the creek petered out in a swampy area. The ground was spongy, and there were many small springs and rivulets. And here, for a couple of hundred feet, were some different kinds of vegetation: watercress, cattails, ferns, and long veils of green moss trailed from the tree branches.

Ben unclipped the hound's leash. She ran around the area, nose down, for about ten minutes, but could not pick up the scent.

"Well, hell," Stuart said.

Ben lit a cigarette.

"What now, Ben?"

"It'll be getting dark soon. We'll go down to that last clearing and bivouac."

"Ben, are you sure you want to spend the night out?"

"We have to. It would take us six hours to get back up here tomorrow morning. We've got to kill that leopard."

"Maybe he'll just crawl off somewhere and die on his own."

"And maybe not."

"Ben, if that hound can't find any scent now, what makes you think she'll be able to tomorrow morning?"

"This rain will turn into snow when the temperature drops a few more degrees," Ben said. "If that cat is anywhere around in the morning, we'll find his track."

"Christ."

"You wounded that leopard with your Robin Hood set, Stuart. Now we've got to kill him before he eats a hippie backpacker or a hunter or some kids."

Bernard was kneeling on the ground forty feet away.

"Find anything?" Ben asked.

The Indian stiffly got to his feet and walked toward them. "Cat, Ben. Not leopard—the little cat—remember?"

"I remember. How old is the sign?"

"Not old."

Ben slowly shook his head. "Do you suppose . . . ?"

Bernard shrugged.

Stuart swore softly.

"Do you suppose that the hound got switched off onto the mountain lion's trail?"

"I think maybe so, Ben."

"Of course she did," Stuart said in disgust.

"Then where, gentlemen, is our leopard?"

They retreated down the muddy path. Ben decided that the best bivouac site would be next to the creek in the center of the clearing. The leopard would have to cross at least forty-five feet of open ground to reach them. He did not expect it to attack; it would naturally try to escape from the humans who had hurt it. And yet, it was a leopard, a great leopard, an unpredictable animal under normal circumstances; now wounded, and now free after a lifetime spent in cages. They would be stupid to take chances.

When they reached the clearing he sent Bernard off to gather wood for a fire. Stuart went along to stand guard.

Ben removed two telescoping aluminum poles from his rucksack, extended them to their full length, then drove the thick ends into the ground eight feet apart. The nylon tarp was eight feet wide and twelve feet long. He attached one end of the tarp to the poles, then stretched the other end out and pegged it to the ground with three aluminum stakes. He used some elastic cord to tighten it even more. When he finished the raindrops bounced off the taut nylon with a drumming sound. The lean-to was open at the west and along the slanting sides. Ben figured that the wind would continue to blow down-valley through the night, and they would be protected from the worst of the wind and rain.

Bernard dumped a pile of twigs and small branches on the ground. He had collected them in the forest, beneath the canopy of trees, and they were fairly dry.

"We're going to need enough wood to last all night," Ben said.

"That right, Ben," the Indian said, and he turned and walked a few paces, hesitated, then jumped the creek.

Ben collected a few dozen of the small twigs. He carefully built a little pyramid of twigs over three candle stubs, lit the wicks, and protected the structure from the wind and rain. The damp wood steamed, sputtered softly, and then took fire. Bernard returned with a load of larger branches. Ben gradually added more twigs to the fire, some small branches, and when he calculated the fire was hot enough he added several logs as long and thick as his forearm. He extended the fire in a line about ten feet from the opening of the lean-to. The tarp would act as a sort of reflector oven; they should be warm enough tonight.

Bernard and Stuart returned with more wood. Stuart now wore his rifle in a shoulder sling.

"You might keep that thing ready," Ben said.

"The dog doesn't smell anything. The cat's not around, Ben."

They left.

Ben got a three-quart aluminum pot from his rucksack and half filled it with water from the creek. He threw in some bouillon cubes, a sliced onion, a handful of quick rice, a can of Spam cut into inch-square cubes, a large potato, also cubed, several small green chili peppers, a packet of dehydrated chicken noodle soup, salt and pepper, and all that remained of a bottle of catsup. He wished he had been more selective in raiding the kitchen, but he really hadn't believed it would be necessary to spend the night out.

He took a stick and dragged some coals out of the fire. He formed them into a bed a few inches thick and fifteen inches in diameter, then set the pot on top.

Bernard and Stuart arrived with another load of wood.

"What is that slop?" Stuart asked.

"I call it stew."

"Glad I'm hungry," Stuart said.

Ben went with them to gather more wood. They made half a dozen trips into the forest.

"Think that's enough?" Stuart asked.

"Should be."

Stuart dragged one of the weather-sculpted white logs close to the fire and sat down. His clothes began to steam.

"I got to crap, Ben," Bernard said.

"You have my permission, Bernard."

Bernard grinned crookedly. "Got paper, Ben?"

"No."

Bernard shrugged, picked up his shotgun, and turned.

"Take my shotgun, Bernard. You'll have two shots if you need them. And take the dog."

Bernard set his shotgun against a log, picked up Ben's, jumped the creek, and started off toward the trees.

"He's a tough old man to be doing this at his age," Stuart said.

"Would you like a drink, Stuart?"

"Have you got something?"

"I put a fifth of brandy and some aluminum cups in your rucksack. Get them out and we'll have a quick one."

Stuart unbuckled the straps on the flap of the rucksack, removed the bottle and two cups. "What about the Indian? Shouldn't we wait for him?"

"No, he can't have any. We'll have to sneak it. If he gets a taste of the stuff he'll fall off the wagon."

"Can't handle it, huh?"

"He can go six months, a year without drinking, but just give him one drink and he's off on a two-week binge."

"Indians just can't drink," Stuart said.

"Some can, some can't. Bernard can't. I've started to think that maybe I can't either."

Stuart broke the seal on the brandy bottle and poured a few ounces into the cups. "Creek water?"

"Not for the first one."

Stuart handed him a cup. "Cheers."

"Cheers," Ben said, and he drank the brandy.

Stuart took Ben's cup and poured in more brandy. "Want water in it now?"

"No, I'll take it straight again, let it burn."

"What do you think about that leopard, Ben?"

"I think he turned off and went back to the cliffs. That's rough country, natural cat country back there."

Stuart sipped his brandy. "I'm glad you brought this stuff," he said. "Christ, I was cold. The rain's letting up now, too. This will be a decent little camp if it stops raining."

"I think it'll probably rain or snow most of the night."

"Well, that's okay. If it does, it does. At first, you know, I was a little dubious about camping out, but now I'm glad. I need this, Ben. I like it. I think the only time I'm really alive is when I'm outdoors, hunting or fishing. Ben, I get along good in Dallas. I make money. I've got friends. I can sit down to table with a Hunt or Murchison and not feel uncomfortable. I've come far. But it isn't like this. I've made enough money for ten lifetimes. I'm forty-four years old, fat, out of shape, I've got high blood pressure. I don't want any more of that life. I like this country, Ben."

"It's good country."

"I want to rest. I'm tired, Ben. I want a place for Meredith and Peter and me."

"This country is going fast," Ben said, "like every other place. But it may last my lifetime. I've given up caring what comes after."

"I don't like people who talk about artificiality," Stuart said. "This is artificial, that's artificial. My life has been real enough, I've made a contribution.

Nothing artificial about the work I've done and the life I've led. I just want something else now."

"I want the same things I've always had," Ben said.

"Here comes the Indian."

"Drink up, Stuart. Hide the bottle."

When the stew was ready Ben carved six slices of bread off a round Spanish loaf, and they sat on the white log, plates balanced on their knees, looking into the fire as they ate. The dog lay between them and the fire, begging with her eyes. When they had finished eating, Ben broke up the rest of the bread, mixed it in with what remained of the stew, and gave it to the hound.

It was dusk now, a few minutes away from night. They could hear the faint squeaking of bats. The surrounding trees and hills gradually receded into the darkness. They sat together on the log for a half-hour, and then the rain changed to snow. It was cold beyond the perimeter of the fire's heat.

"I'm beat," Stuart said. "Guess I'll try to sleep for a while."

"We might as well keep watches," Ben said. "Just in case. Bernard, you take the first, okay? I'll take the second. Stuart, you take the third. Four hours each—that should take us to dawn."

"You don't really believe that leopard will come around, do you, Ben?" Stuart asked.

"I don't think he will," Ben said. "But I don't know that he won't."

Stuart crawled into the lean-to.

Ben got up, added some heavy logs to the fire, then again sat down on the log. "Stuart?" he said.

"Yeah?"

"I've been thinking. Your idea—what you suggested the other day? Maybe we can make a deal. We'll form a kind of corporation and I'll sell you forty-nine percent of the ranch. I guess there's no other way I can manage."

There was a long silence. "Fifty percent, Ben."

"I'll think about it."

Sixteen

*T*om Stuart did not expect to sleep. He was wet, cold, the ground was hard and lumpy beneath the foam pad, and he was still keyed up from the hunt; but his fatigue overcame all those things and he was soon asleep. He awoke once—minutes later? hours?—and saw the Indian standing by the fire, and heard Ben's deep breathing next to him, and then he dozed off again. His dreams were vague and empty of people; he dreamed of country, climate: sun-glazed summer days, balmy blue twilights, a muddy brown river, seas of winter wheat stretching off to a hair-thin horizon, sunsets like old bruises. Nothing happened in his dreams. He did not appear. A part of his mind was aware that he was dreaming, that he was a *child* dreaming—the adult Thomas Stuart had not yet evolved. And so he dreamed, a boy again, nostalgic for an even earlier time.

There was something heavy on his chest. Stinking wet fur, throaty moans, hot breath on his face. He cried out and pushed the weight away.

Laughter. Ben, a shadow against the fire. There was snow on the ground, and thick snowflakes falling obliquely through the light.

"The goddamned *dog* crawled on top of me," Stuart said. His voice sounded all right, low enough, and he did not hurry the words.

Ben laughed again. "I think the leopard is somewhere out there."

"How do you know?"

"The way the hound has been behaving the last twenty minutes. Anxious, whining, smelling the air, trying to crawl up on my lap. I wouldn't let her, so she crawled onto you."

"Brave dog."

"I'm a little scared myself," Ben said.

"What time is it?"

"Just about time for your watch. Ten to three."

Stuart crawled stiffly out of the lean-to. There was five inches of snow on the ground.

"Christ," he said.

"There's water boiling, if you want coffee."

"How long do you expect this snow'll last, Ben?"

"A while. It isn't near ready to quit."

Stuart got his tin cup, spooned in some instant coffee, and filled the cup with hot water.

"Ben?"

"It's in your rucksack."

Stuart poured an ounce of brandy into his cup, then

brushed snow off the log and sat down next to Ben. His body ached. He was still tired, his eyes were sore and gummy, and a chalky-tasting scum coated his tongue. He sipped the coffee. It was uncomfortably warm this close to the fire, but Stuart felt a coldness within, as if the cold of the ground had gradually seeped into his bones. He felt both cold and hot now.

"Shit," he said.

Ben, the shotgun balanced across his knees, was looking out into the darkness.

"Ben, what if he comes up behind us?"

"He won't come downwind."

"Why not?"

"Because he'd think we could smell him. Predators hunt upwind or crosswind."

"Yeah, but, Ben, we're humans, we can't smell that good."

"The leopard doesn't know that."

Stuart resisted the impulse to turn and look over his shoulder. "I saw lions hunt downwind in Africa."

"You saw team ambushes. The lions deliberately move downwind of a herd to spook them with their smell. The lionesses are waiting below to make the kill. Wolves sometimes hunt the same way, I've heard. But a single cat is going to attack upwind or crosswind. It's instinct with them."

Stuart blew on the coffee, shifted his weight. "Ben, you said the dog was nervous."

"Scared half to death."

"Well, then she must have scented the cat. The cat must have been above us."

"Yeah."

"Well?"

"I think he was probably trying to panic us with his smell. Get us to run off into the darkness, where we'd be easy."

"Ben, I surely do hope that cat isn't as smart as you think he is."

"They've had millions of years to get smart."

"And you really think that cat is hunting *us*?"

"I do."

"What about the fire?"

"I don't think the fire as such worries him. He's seen Bernard build fifty campfires. It's the light, I think. He doesn't want to come into the light, where we can see him."

"Now, Ben, you don't know that the cat is out there, do you?"

"No, I don't."

"You're just guessing that he is because of the way the bitch is acting."

"That's right."

"And you think he's going to attack."

"No, I doubt very much he will. He'd rather scare us out into the darkness."

"Okay, Ben. No offense, Ben, but I think you're full of shit. Why don't you go to sleep now. I'll take over."

"Here's the shotgun."

"Ben, you know that if that cat is out there, and if he decides to come, this shotgun won't be worth beans. He'd be all over me before I'd know he was here."

"I know," Ben said grinning. "Why don't you give me your .357. I could shoot him off your back."

Stuart withdrew his revolver from the holster and

handed it to Ben. "Are you trying to scare me?" he asked.

"I wouldn't waste any time trying to scare a Texan. I know for a fact that Texans don't scare. Any number of Texans have assured me they're fearless."

"Go to bed," Stuart said. "And don't mess with the Indian, Ben."

Ben grinned at him.

"He's an old man, none too clean."

"Don't you mess with the dog," Ben said.

"The dog's female. That's a different thing altogether."

Ben stood up. "Wake me up at first light."

"Okay."

"I'll drag the hound off of my bed and tie her to the log. You can watch her and get an idea what's going on out there in the darkness. She's got a good nose, and she can hear much better than us."

"You trust me alone with her, Ben?"

Ben dragged the dog out of the lean-to, clipped the leash chain onto her collar, and secured the other end to the log. The hound was trembling; she grinned at Stuart, thumped her tail in the snow, then lowered her head and crawled closer to the fire.

"Shit eater," Stuart said.

"First light," Ben said from the lean-to.

Stuart broke open the shotgun, pulled the shells and examined them, returned them to the chambers, and closed the action.

Imagine that Pearce trying to scare me with a lot of smoke about the leopard being out there and hunting us. I can take that kind of kidding, but I don't like it when he turns mean. As soon as you find yourself liking him he becomes sarcastic or tries to run over the top of you with some horseshit command or other. He's got ten moods and you're always running one or two moods behind him. He's natural and friendly and droll and you find yourself opening up to him, feeling good, and then the son of a bitch double-crosses you and turns cold mean.

I had to warn him away from Meredith. I saw her heating him up. She promises a new dimension in sex. Now there ain't any new dimensions, but she gets so intense, so *anguished*, that she makes men believe that there might be. I don't want to know if they were together last night. They probably were. But if they were, I don't want to know for sure. I can't take much more, I've been carrying this misery too long . . . I might do something bad if I knew for sure they had been together. It scares me, what I might do.

The fact is that sex doesn't mean much to Meredith. She's a cold woman that way, always was, is now. There's no pleasure in it for her. Sex is a way of expressing something other than pleasure or love for Meredith—rebellion, contempt, loathing, death. That's what the doctors say. Your wife is essentially a frigid woman, the doctors told me, even the one who was screwing her every chance he got. The doctors are confident men and they have all kinds of theories and therapies, but they can't help her. They really don't know what they're doing. Each one has a different diagnosis and a different prognosis. They remind me of the mystics that Meredith used to bring home, the palm readers, mediums, astrologers. The psychiatrists I've met have the same air of smug certainty and the pathetic faith that to describe something in scientific or pseudo-scientific jargon is to master that thing. The doctors were wonderful at writing twenty-five page reports on Mere's sickness, but the trouble was that Mere was not there when they finished. They described a disease, maybe accurately, maybe even beautifully, but the patient had somehow gotten lost in the process. They weren't treating Meredith Stuart, they were treating chronic schizophrenia.

One time I finished reading one of the evaluation reports and I said, "Fine, now where's my wife?" The doctor didn't understand. He said, "She's in her room."

Poor Mere. She'll have to be confined again. Maybe I was wrong to have her released. It might be best for her, and for Peter and me, if she were kept in an institution for the rest of her life. But how can you do that? How can you entrust her to the care of such people?

Stuart tossed a small log on the fire. It was a big fire and threw light for twenty-five feet before being turned back by the darkness. The down-valley breeze curved the flames, causing the shadows along the perimeter of light to stretch and shrink plastically. Snow was still falling.

Peter. She's infected him. I've got to get the boy away from her. From me, too. I'll send him away to some good boarding school.

The dog was lying quietly, muzzle resting on extended forepaws, eyes open. Her eyes were turned upward and to the side, watching Stuart. She seemed calm enough now. I'll rely on the dog to warn me if the leopard is upwind, he thought. Ben was right about that. But he was wrong when he talked about relying on the dog's superior hearing, too; cats don't make much noise, especially on snow. And anyway, the creek would cover any sounds the cat did make.

The wind gusted, fluttering the tips of the flames and tearing a spiral of orange sparks from the fire. Stuart watched the sparks swirl off into the darkness.

He estimated that an hour had passed. Ben and the Indian were sleeping. Ben was a strange guy. The Indian was stupid. If he was white everyone would realize that he was a moron, but he was Indian and so it was necessary to pretend that he was just the product of a different, though equal or even superior, culture. The fact was that he was a nice old guy, but stupid. Stuart thought that if one had to be stupid it was just as well nowadays to be an Indian or Negro or Arab or something. You could talk any kind of horseshit at all and people would listen respectfully.

The dog was still watching him. The shit eater was flat-out scared. Well, why not? She'd been there when that leopard was moving around like a buzz saw.

I'll take a quick piss and then have another cup of coffee with brandy in it.

He stiffly got to his feet, cocked both hammers on the shotgun, and moved away from the camp. He held the shotgun at waist level with his right hand, and with his left hand unzipped his fly and urinated into the snow. It was very cold away from the fire; the moisture in his nostrils froze, and he exhaled great clouds of vapor. Snow, red-tinted from the firelight, hazed the air. He zipped his fly. There were dark spots on the snow over there on the other side of the creek. Without thinking about it, reacting with an impulsive fear-anger, he jumped the creek and walked off into the shadows. Cat tracks, bigger than the palm of his hand. He felt a cold, prickly sensation on his arms and shoulders. He turned, ran a few yards, jumped the creek, and returned to the fire. The dog was sitting up now, watching him. The fur along her spine bristled, and she whined softly She had sensed his fear.

Jesus! The leopard had been within thirty-five feet of the camp and he'd been daydreaming.

The cat has been moving around out there in the darkness, watching me.

Wake Ben and the Indian?

No, calm down, think about it. Maybe those are the tracks of the young mountain lion.

Like hell!

I wish that goddamned dog would stop looking at me like I'm God. She's trying to smell the air, she looks desperate. It's the fire, the smoke, of course; the smoke has ruined her sense of smell.

Wake Ben.

No, I can't do that. Ben knew the cat was out there earlier tonight and he didn't wake me. And then he trusted me enough to go to sleep. This is my job, it's my duty to protect the people here. Stop turning around in circles, slow down, think. Assume that the leopard is watching.

"Okay," he said softly.

More wood for the fire. More light. Move very slowly, the cat is out there watching; if I move jerkily, unnaturally, he'll understand. Easy, move slow, here's a good piece. Another. Christ, is there enough wood to keep the fire going until morning? Say something. Say something slow and quiet.

He turned and looked out into the darkness. There, a shadow, eyes? He lifted the shotgun, aimed, and felt the coldness of the trigger on his finger. He lowered the gun.

"Easy, dog," he said softly. "Just take it easy now, it's okay."

He stood very straight, expanded his chest, lifted his shoulders; he was a big man, let the cat see just how big.

The dog was pulling at the chain. She flicked her ears, whined, lifted her head and expanded her nostrils.

I'm a big man, let the cat see. Move slow; confident animals move slow and calm, nothing threatens them

"It's okay," he whispered to the dog.

The dog had apparently caught the leopard's scent; she whined, turned her raised muzzle from side to side, and then slowly, submissively lowered her belly to the ground.

There was a sound then. It came from upstream and sounded close. There was a kind of coughing noise, as if an animal had a bone in its throat; a low choking, and then a noise that was a combination of choking, snarling, and hissing—a deep, though not loud, exhalation.

The dog leaped to her feet, backed, shaking her head, until she came loose from the collar, and then she jumped the creek and raced off into the darkness.

Ben's voice, slurred with sleep: "Everything all right?"

"Just fine, Ben," Stuart drawled. How could he sleep through this?

Stuart heard the leopard often that night, each time from a different direction. The cat stayed just beyond the perimeter of firelight. He moved around in the darkness, snarling softly, coughing, hissing, and Stuart felt the fear building inside him. He had experienced an equal fear in his life, but never of this duration; this went on for three hours, and all that time he believed that the leopard might attack at any moment. The fear exhausted him; he had never been so tired. He knew that he could dilute his fear, share it, by waking Ben and the Indian, but he refused to do that. Ben had not wakened him. The Indian had not wakened him. Each had assumed the full responsibility of sentry duty. It was a simple matter of honor to refuse to ask for help. It was his duty to protect the camp.

Seventeen

Ben dreamed that he was searching through the rooms of a big house. He was looking for some-one, but he did not know whom, nor for what pur-pose; he felt sure that he would recognize the person and his mission when the time came. The rooms were all the same size and shape, perfect squares, and empty of furniture. The house had not been occupied for years; there was a musty odor of dust and dry rot and rat droppings, and cold night wind blew in through the broken windows. He wandered down long dark corridors, ascended and descended stair-ways to other floors, examined rooms which led to identical rooms which led to still more rooms.

It was just beginning to get light when he awak-ened. Bernard, snoring softly, his mouth open, was lying next to him. Stuart sat on the log in front of the fire. Ben unrolled his poncho and crawled out of the lean-to.

Stuart turned. "Morning, Ben."

"Good morning." Ben felt that his sleep, though long and deep enough, had tired rather than refreshed him. He was cold, and his body ached. His eyes were gummy. He stood up and looked around the clearing. There was six or seven inches of snow on the ground, but it was not snowing now. Details were blurred in the soft, filmy light. The fire had burned down to a mound of orange coals and a single transparent leaf of flame. Charcoaled wood and soot and ashes stained the snow.

"Christ," Ben said. He was groggy; his legs were weak.

Stuart grinned at him.

Ben carried the small saucepan to the creek and dipped it in the water. He could see the colored pebbles on the bottom and the ridged patterns the current had raised in the sandy places. The above-surface dome of a boulder had been glazed with a half-inch-thick layer of clear ice. He straightened and started to turn, then saw the tracks in the snow.

"Jesus, Stuart."

"What is it?"

"That leopard came close enough to spit on us last night."

"What? Oh, yeah, he hung around camp for several hours. He left just before it got light enough to shoot."

"Why didn't you wake me?"

"What would you have done, Ben?"

"I don't know. Vomited, maybe."

Ben returned and placed the saucepan of water on the hot coals. He glanced sideways at Stuart. The big man was tired; he was pale, loose-skinned, puffy around the eyes.

"As soon as it started getting light I went out there," Stuart said. "There's a little blood on the snow, not much."

Ben shook his head.

"There are tracks all around us, on all sides. I think the cat wanted to come in here after us, but he didn't have quite enough nerve."

"Did that leopard make any noise last night?"

"He did, Ben. I'll say he did."

"Christ, and I thought I was dreaming it."

"He came close, real close."

"You should have got me up. Where's the dog?"

"She couldn't take it—she slipped free of her collar and ran."

"Oh, shit," Ben said.

"That dog is no good."

"We needed her nose."

"That Airedale was a real dog, but the hound doesn't have any heart."

"Stuart, the hound gave us an extra sense. Two. She could have picked up the airborne scent of the cat, and she can hear better than us. Now we've only got our eyes, and the leopard will run us off into the thick brush. . . . Bernard, get your lazy ass out of there!" Ben kicked the pan of water. It bounced over the snow, rolled into the creek, and was swept downstream. "Son of a bitch! Bows and arrows, huh, Stuart?"

"Take it easy, Ben."

"Bernard!"

"Okay, Ben, okay," Bernard said, crawling out of the lean-to.

"And now the dog's gone, Stuart, and you tell me we don't need her."

"That's enough now, Ben."

Bernard remained on his hands and knees for a moment and then stiffly, pausing between each separate stage, got to his feet.

"Let's go," Ben said. "Now. Leave this stuff here, just bring the guns."

"I think I stay here, Ben," Bernard said.

Ben turned. "What did you say?"

"I had bad dreams, Benny."

"Oh, Jesus Christ!"

"Leave him alone," Stuart said.

"You had bad dreams, did you, Bernard?"

"Real bad."

"Did the spirits send you a message, Bernard?" Ben said furiously. "Did the goddamned mountain ring your number?"

"My bones hurt, Ben. Arthritis—they hurt."

"The spirits never ring me up, Bernard. So I've got to go out there and hunt down that leopard."

"Ben," Stuart drawled softly, "leave him alone."

"He's coming with us."

"He's too old for this, Ben. Let him be."

"Did the spirits tell you to take his side, Stuart?"

"Ben, he's old. Three are too many, anyhow— we'd just get in each other's way."

"Okay," Ben said.

"He'll just get in our way."

"All right," Ben said. "Let's go then."

"I'm ready. I doubt if I've ever been more ready."

"I'll carry this rucksack. Bernard, pack up all the other stuff and donkey it down."

"Sure, Ben."

The leopard had gone downstream. There was not much blood, little starbursts of bright red scattered here and there over the snow, but the animal had been bleeding that way for many hours now and it had to have weakened him. The cat moved in a series of bounds, rear and front paws close together, stopped to rest, then went on again in the same way. Two hundred yards below camp there was a depression in the snow where the leopard had lain.

Ben and Stuart went slowly down the trail, scanning the trees and brush around them. Ben had cocked the hammers of his shotgun. He assumed that Stuart's rifle was ready to be fired.

It was cold. The snow was light and dry, and compressed underfoot with a squeaking sound. Thin streams of powdery snow hissed down through the tree branches. The light gradually increased, but perspective remained poor; nearly everything was a uniform grayish-white, the sky, the ground, the snow-heavy trees, and there were no shadows. The landscape reminded Ben of an overexposed photograph, without real definition or dimension. They moved cautiously, examining each potential ambush site— the leopard could come at them from just about anywhere.

Ben went first, following the cat's footprints. The tracks in the snow united them, bound them together in a tender and cruel intimacy. Something about this day seemed inevitable. His life and the leopard's life converged at a point not far away in space or time. How had they come to oppose each other?

Then he saw motion out of the corner of his eye, a dark blur against the snow. It was about forty yards away and coming fast. He whirled, raised the shotgun with his finger hooked around the triggers, aimed— but it was the hound. She bounded toward them, leaped against Ben's leg, leaped again, and then did a quick little dance of contrition and shame in the snow.

"I almost fired on her," Stuart said.

"So did I."

"I had her lined up."

"This is kind of hard on the nerves."

"You ain't lying, Ben."

Ben leaned down and petted the dog. "Spent a cold night, huh?"

"Cold and lonely and scary," Stuart said. "And no sleep. That leopard—it seems like there must be a hundred crazy leopards out here, one behind every tree. Hell, they can climb like squirrels—up in every tree, too. I got little leopards crawling up and down my spine, Ben. And I got dust-speck-sized leopards running back and forth behind my eyes."

Ben grinned.

"I got a gutful of leopards turning my shit to water."

"Well, the leopard isn't in this immediate vicinity or else the dog wouldn't have come out of hiding. We can relax for a few minutes."

"Relax, huh? I don't think so."

Ben got out his package of cigarettes, shook one loose, lit it, and deeply inhaled.

"It's winter," Stuart said. "Yesterday was like a day in early June, now it's January. Do you think it'll clear up?"

"I don't know. It probably will before tonight."

"I believe I'd like a belt of that brandy."

"The brandy is back in camp."

"It isn't in your rucksack?"

"No, I grabbed the wrong one."

"I could have used some. I'm cold, inside and out."

"I'm sorry. I meant to bring it, but I grabbed the wrong rucksack. I didn't want to leave it behind for Bernard to find."

"It's probably just as well, Ben."

"Right, it wouldn't do you any good."

"That bottle's no doubt full of nasty little leopards by now."

Ben looked at him. The big man was nervous, maybe more than a little frightened, but he was cheerful too. Sort of anarchistically happy, the way some men get when there is danger. Ben assumed that Stuart felt now as Ben himself had felt yesterday just after the leopard had been wounded. Ben remembered that he hadn't been able to stop grinning afterward. He wished that he felt the same way this morning. Now he was aware only of the cold and his fatigue and fear. Fear without exhilaration was dread, a dirty thing; it had a sour smell and it tasted like bile. It made you slow, gloomy. But there was another kind of fear too, which quickened you, liberated you as nothing else could.

"Feeling pretty cocky this morning, huh?" Ben said.

"I don't know, Ben. What do you think?"

"Try and stay cocky. This may be a long day."

"It can't be any longer than last night."

"Puff out your chest a little more and you won't be able to see where you're walking."

Stuart smiled at him.

"That leopard will probably break down and cry when he sees big Tom Stuart strutting his way."

Stuart laughed. "Come on, Ben, enough. You woke up mean and you're getting meaner every minute."

"Let's see if the dog is willing to go to work." Ben started down the trail; Stuart followed a few yards behind. The hound remained still for a moment, watching them, and then she whined, got up, and bounded past them.

The high winds had ripped a hole in the cloud cover; the hole was elongated into a seam that ran half the width of the sky, then it began peeling back, exposing the dark vibrant blue. Sunlight sprayed down through the trees and struck prismatic sparks from the snow crystals. Shadows bloomed.

Another mile downstream they saw where the leopard had paused to drink from the creek, and then leaped to the opposite bank and headed off through the trees toward the cliff country.

Ben brushed the snow off a fallen tree and sat down. The hound sprawled out in the snow and began gnawing at the ice balls that had formed between the pads of her paws.

"What do you think?" Stuart asked.

"I think it's going to be a bitch."

Stuart nodded. "It looks like rough country back there."

"It is."

"Maybe we should have brought the other dogs."

"Probably so."

Stuart, his legs spread, the rifle balanced lightly on his shoulder, looked down at the creek. "It's at least twelve feet from bank to bank here."

"Yeah," Ben said.

"Twelve feet, possibly a little more. That leopard leaped twelve feet from a standing start and landed as gentle as a snowflake."

"That cat can do anything he wants to do. He can write letters to our next of kin tonight if he's in the mood."

Stuart smiled. "You aren't enjoying this much."

"Not much."

"I am. Really, Ben, that's no lie. I'm getting pleasure out of this."

"You won't be quite so fired up when you see the country we're going into."

"I'm hungry and cold, and I'm still tired from yesterday, but I feel good. Real good. This is hunting, this is the real thing."

"Yeah?" Ben said.

"There is something basic about hunting, Ben, something true."

"Something—elemental," Ben said.

"That's right, elemental."

"Shit," Ben said.

"I don't mind saying that I was scared last night."

"Is that so?"

"I'm not now. But last night . . . Maybe it was the

dark. That leopard was so aggressive, Ben, so hating. He loathes us."

"He's got the right."

"You don't expect any animal to behave the way he did. Prowling around the fire all night, just out of sight in the shadows, circling and making those god-awful noises. Quiet, he wasn't loud, mostly it was like hissing and coughing and groaning. Christ! There were moments when I wanted to bolt like the dog. Just run."

This sounded like the beginning of a confession. Ben hated confessions. He stood up.

"Ben, did you ever have a dentist picking away at a hole in a tooth and strike a nerve? Then you relax and he hits it again. Well, every time that leopard made a sound he struck a nerve. A deep nerve, one that ran all the way through me. Except it wasn't physical, not exactly. It hurt, but I don't know. . . . It was deep, it had been covered up for a long, long time, it was a buried nerve. But that leopard reached down and picked at the nerve, opened it up. I'm not telling this right. I can't, I guess."

"Sure," Ben said.

"That cat kind of took me apart, Ben, and I had to put myself back together again. I was forced to do a kind of visceral thinking, if that makes any sense."

Ben's patience broke. "Stuart, just what is the point of all this? There's something we've got to do, man—we can't stay here all day playing penitent and priest."

Stuart turned sharply and stared at him. It was a long, cool, appraising stare. There was no hostility in it. Nor any sign of retreat.

"No point," Stuart said finally.

And then Ben realized that he had not been listening to Stuart's confession. The big man had not yet begun to confess. Everything he'd said had merely been the prelude to the confession, the orientation, the background detail. Stuart had not ashamedly been admitting to his terror of last night; the terror had been the trigger of an insight. And Ben had perhaps interrupted him. It was just as well. Let the thing grow a bit before exposing it to the light and heat.

Ben stood up. "We'll hunt the cat until about three this afternoon, and if we don't get him by then we'll start down. I can try to borrow some dogs tonight, good lion dogs. Tomorrow we'll try again."

"We *are* going to get him today, Ben. I can feel it."

Eighteen

S it down and have breakfast with us," Mrs. Stuart said.

"I'll just have coffee," Anita Jaramillo replied. "I'm not hungry right now." She was hungry, but she did not like to eat in front of other people, especially strangers. Her dentures did not fit properly, they slipped, she could not trust them, and it was always an embarrassment to chew food in front of others, even food as soft as fried eggs and hash browns. She would eat later, when Meredith Stuart and her son had left the kitchen. She'd remove her dentures, it was easier to eat without them. And you could taste the food better.

"My, it's still snowing," Mrs. Stuart said.

Anita poured a little water into the frying pan that

contained the eggs and quickly clamped on the cover to trap the steam.

"I'll bet the men spent an awful miserable night."

Anita turned. Mrs. Stuart and her son were sitting side by side at the table, heads cocked sideways to watch the snow falling past the window. It had rained most of the night, was sleeting when Anita got up at dawn, soon after turned to snow, and now the ground was covered with a smooth layer of white.

"Hard on all of them," Mrs. Stuart went on, "but especially for that poor old man."

She seemed younger this morning: younger and gentler and more relaxed. And her voice was a soft lilting drawl, but without that queer whispery quality. Anita unwillingly found herself half liking Meredith Stuart this morning, and feeling sorry for her, but not trusting her. No, you could never trust that one.

"Although it hasn't been too very cold, has it?"

"It's colder up high," Anita said, removing the lid from the frying pan and setting it aside. "And there'll be more snow up there."

"But I mean, there isn't any danger, is there? They wouldn't freeze or anything?"

"No."

"And they couldn't get lost, could they?"

"No, no, there's no chance of that." Anita filled two plates with eggs, hash brown potatoes, and bacon, and carried them over to the table.

"It's so vast up there, so confusing."

Anita turned the coffee cups right side up and poured in coffee, then sat down across from Mrs. Stuart.

"Ben and Bernard couldn't get lost up there if they

tried," she said. "They know these mountains like you know your face."

The boy was pale, as always, and there were dark patches beneath his eyes. She had heard him quietly sobbing last night at around midnight—their rooms were adjacent—but he seemed cheerful enough this morning. He had teased her when he first came into the kitchen, imitating her accent, but in an affectionate way. He'd actually been smart-alecky, which was never a bad sign in an adolescent boy, and was positively a sign of health in this one.

Now Peter put three teaspoons of sugar in his coffee and stirred it. "Don't worry, Mother," he said. "Our intrepid heroes are probably enjoying their suffering. They're outdoorsmen, aren't they? You can't be an outdoorsman without anguish, can you?"

Meredith Stuart smiled briefly.

"They've got lots of hair on their chests to keep them warm and dry," Peter said. He began eating.

Anita watched the boy break off a piece of toast and delicately dip it into the yolk of one of his eggs. She was amused by the way he ate breakfast: he very neatly soaked up all of the yolks with toast, and when he was finished the two perfect egg whites, sockets empty, remained on the plate.

"I know a man," Anita said, "who eats his egg whites and leaves the yolks. You and he should breakfast together."

"We should, we really should," Peter said. "What is the man's name?"

"Mr. Vida. Jorge Vida."

Peter grinned. "Vida? Doesn't *vida* mean life in Spanish?"

"Yes."

"And that's really his name? Life?"

"Vida. Life, yes."

"And is Life nasty, brutish, and short?"

"He's short. I don't know about the nasty and brutish."

Peter laughed, turned his head. "Mother, when will
you get your new car?"

"What new car?"

"Isn't father going to buy you a new car?"

"No, he hasn't said anything."

"He was going to buy me a Jaguar automobile for
killing the jaguar cat. To be consistent he should buy
you a new Cougar for killing the cougar."

"We have enough cars," Meredith said.

"You're a formidable huntress, Mother."

"Peter—"

"A sort of Dallas Diana. Deadly Dallas Diana."

"Peter, I have a slight headache. Don't be witty
with me this morning, dear."

"Mrs. Jaramillo, you should have seen my mother—what's the word Father uses? Bust?—bust that
mountain lion. Boy, did she ever bust it! Life is, ah,
a fragile entity, is it not, Mrs. Jaramillo?"

"Short, nasty, brutal, and fragile," Anita said.

"Touché!" Peter cried, laughing. "Hoist by my
own petard."

"You're talking like an old movie this morning,"
Anita said.

"Mother, aren't you going to eat your eggs?"

"No."

"May I have them?"

"Of course, dear."

Peter took his mother's plate, broke off a piece of toast, dipped it into a yolk, lifted it to his mouth, and chewed slowly. "I hope I don't OD on cholesterol. Mother, do you think I'm a latent homosexual?"

"What?"

"Do you?"

"Peter, please, for God's sake."

"Father does."

"He doesn't think any such thing."

"He's afraid I'm going to turn into a flaming faggot. Peter the Queen. Admit it, Mother."

"Peter, stop tormenting me."

"It's hormonal, Mother. I was born that way. Will you loan me the money for a sex-change operation?"

"Peter . . ."

He smiled at Anita. "Mrs. Jaramillo, do you find me grossly effeminate?"

"Of course not," she said.

"What am I, Mrs. Jaramillo? I respect your practical nature, your honest opinions."

"You're an adolescent boy, Peter," Anita said. "That isn't a good thing to be, but it doesn't last very long."

He nodded and smiled. "Would you say that I'm a punk, then?"

"No."

"A brat?"

"You're a brat this morning, all right."

"But I mean, would you trust me with your motorcycle?"

"Peter," Meredith said, "you're being very rude. Harass me, if you feel you must, but leave Mrs. Jaramillo alone."

"Mother, tell me, why did you marry Father?"

"Please, Peter, some other time."

"I mean, did you love him?"

"Why, of course I did."

"Do you still love him?"

"Peter, really—"

"Was it a beauty-and-the-beast attraction? Fay Wray and King Kong, the princess and the frog, that kind of thing? You're so ethereal, Mother, so vulnerable and otherworldly—spooky, actually—and Father's . . . well, he's Father. What a clash of genes! And I am the product of your mutual lust."

"Your father has been good to me, Peter."

"How can you say that?"

"It's true."

"It isn't true at all!"

"He's been good to both of us in his way."

"In his way!" Peter said, flushing. "What does that mean?"

"The way he has to be because of who he is, the only way he can be. Like I've been bad in my way."

"Listen," Peter said softly, fiercely, "I hope he dies! I hope that leopard tears out his guts and eats them."

"Oh, Peter," Meredith said sadly, looking down at her hands. "You don't mean that."

"I mean it."

"Now that's enough, Peter," Anita said. "You've upset your mother, you're beginning to upset me, and I want you to leave this kitchen right now."

He looked at her.

"I'm not joking. Now, Peter, go before I chase you out with a broom."

He abruptly rose to his feet, glanced down at his mother, turned, and left the room.

"He didn't mean that," Meredith said.

"I know he didn't mean it. They're all savages at that age. Their glands are driving them crazy."

"He's always been such a sweet boy."

"Sure, and he'll grow up to be a nice man. But now he's got swollen glands, and he's mean and miserable and selfish, a savage. Don't let him upset you."

Meredith smiled. "I feel all right," she said. "I'm strong today. When I'm strong it seems like I'll never be weak again. But the strength doesn't last—I'll be weak again."

"We are all weak sinners," Anita said.

"There is so much pain, so much."

"I'll wash the dishes, you dry. And then we'll clean the whole house, and afterward we'll cook a big hot meal for the men. If you keep busy and work hard you don't think about pain."

Nineteen

The horseshoe-shaped valley was small, no more than three miles long and two miles wide, and it was bordered on the north, east, and west by steep granite cliffs. This basin collected and held water—rain and snowmelt—and the valley floor was thickly forested with fir and spruce and the white columnar aspens. A rust-colored mossy growth had killed many of the trees; some remained standing, others had fallen to horizontal positions, and more had been caught at various angles by the surrounding trees. There was a lot of underbrush too—willow, alder, blueberry, and currant, and a thorny bush that Ben, not knowing the name, had always called thornwhip. It was a dense, tangled patch of forest, gloomy and still. The leopard could be a few yards away and they would not know. The hound's senses were now far more important than their own, especially her sense of smell. They relied on her smelling the cat before it became visible to them.

Ben was sweating despite the cold. He had sweated at intervals since entering the forest two hours ago. Tension had knotted the muscles of his shoulders and lower back. And he had difficulty controlling his breathing; sometimes he abruptly realized that he had been holding his breath for a minute or so; other times he breathed too deeply and rapidly and became dizzy.

Stuart followed close behind. He still seemed quietly elated; he had found it possible to grin at Ben from time to time. Authentic grins too, all of them.

Ben knew that he was incapable of grinning now; he could not even smile, not without looking simpleminded or mad. There was not enough saliva in his mouth to moisten a postage stamp. Smile? He couldn't even swallow. Each of Stuart's grins added to Ben's rage. Where was the humor in crashing through underbrush so thick that you could hardly see your own feet at times, tracking a wounded leopard that might—for Christ's sake—might be coiling to spring out at you right now. And that fat, lighthearted son of a bitch had made it all possible through his pride and stubbornness and sheer stupidity— A bow and arrow, and I let him get away with using it, he thought. He bought me. And what good is that $2,500 bribe going to do me when my guts are spread out on the snow? Do you think Stuart will be there when I need him? If I know anything at all about that Texan, I know that he'll be running the hundred yards in around 9.6 while that leopard is licking my liver preliminary to taking the first bite.

A fallen fir tree, about four feet in diameter, smelling pungently of rot, blocked their way through the woods. Ben could see how the leopard had lightly jumped atop the log and sat there on his haunches for a time before dropping down on the other side. There were a few small splashes of blood on the flattened snow, and a tuft of whitish fur. Probably the animal had licked his wound before going on. Perhaps after that he had lifted his head, ears cocked, nose pulsing, and looked back down the trail. Listening, smelling, watching. Loathing them.

"Watch out now," Ben said softly. He lowered the hammers of his shotgun, swung one leg over the log, sat down briefly, lifted the other leg over, and stood up. He recocked the hammers. The dog jumped up on the log, smelled the blood, and then yawned and whined. "Come on," Ben told the dog. "Okay," he said to Stuart.

The leopard's tracks wandered all over the valley, through the forest, along the rock slabs at the base of the cliff, back into the woods.

Late in the morning the sky clouded over again and it began to snow, lightly at first, then more heavily.

"Ben, let's take a break," Stuart said.

"No, we ought to go on. This snow will cover the tracks."

"Not soon, it won't. I got to thaw out my toes. They've hurt for hours, and now I can't feel them at all."

"Cowboy boots are no good out here."

"Tell me something I don't know."

"Do you want to quit for today, then?" Ben asked, hoping that Stuart would say yes.

"Hell no, I don't want to quit. I only want to stop for fifteen minutes and thaw out my toes."

"Did you wear cowboy boots when you hunted in Africa? Or in Alaska?"

"Ben, stop riding me. You are a spiteful man. Are we going to stop now or not?"

"Not. We'll go on for another hour or so and then rest."

"All right, Ben. Have it your way. I should have insisted that we keep going so that you'd decide to stop."

Toward the end of the valley the leopard crossed his own trail several times, confusing the dog. Ben had to determine which set of tracks appeared freshest, less filled with new snow, and then urge the dog off in the right direction. He wished Bernard were here with them; the old man was slow now, with a sometimes erratic intuition about what the quarry might do, but still a good tracker.

When they were about seventy yards from the rock wall, the fur bristled along the dog's spine; she whined and lowered her tail and turned to look back at Ben.

Ben stopped and waited for Stuart to move next to him. "I think she's got a hot scent," he said softly.

"Looks like it," Stuart whispered.

"There's a small cave up there. Straight ahead and up the incline. The leopard may be laying up inside."

Stuart nodded.

"We'll go on farther, and when I signal—like

this—you stop. I'll circle around to the right and creep in along the base of the cliff and try to spook the cat out."

"I'll go with you."

"No. It's thick up there; the trees and brush run almost up to the cave entrance. And the leopard, if he's in there, will come out like he's on fire. It would be stupid to try this with anything but a shotgun."

"I'll take my revolver. I can handle that at close quarters."

"How about your bow and arrow!" Ben whispered furiously. "Goddamn it, Stuart, listen to me for once—I'll kill him with the shotgun. It's the perfect short-range weapon. I can't miss. But if he somehow does get past me, wounded say, then he'll be coming your direction fast. You'll have a chance to get set, line him up, take him with your rifle."

"It doesn't sound right, Ben. We can do better than this."

"This is the way it's going to be done."

"Give me the shotgun. I'll go up there."

"No."

"I want to, Ben. I wounded the cat. It's my job to go after him."

"No!"

"He's my leopard, by God. I paid for him."

"And you blew it," Ben said. He turned and started off through the brush, moving very slowly, and as quietly as possible, even though he was certain that the leopard was aware of their movements. There was little hope of stalking and surprising that animal. Still, it seemed instinctual, he *had* to move carefully and quietly; he was forced to obey an old imperative.

The incline gradually steepened to about thirty degrees. Ahead, through the trees and the haze of falling snow, Ben could see the lower section of the rock wall. It was a metallic grayish-black in this poor light, with the color and sheen of wet iron. The cave entrance was a dull shadow at the base of the cliff. The leopard's tracks led directly toward it.

Ben stopped and, palm down, made a pumping motion with his hand.

Stuart nodded.

Ben pointed toward the cat's tracks and then the cave, waited for Stuart to nod again, and then he touched himself and drew a half circle in the air.

Stuart lightly slapped the stock of his rifle.

Ben angled off through the trees. The dog followed him for a while and then returned and sprawled in the snow at Stuart's feet.

There was a sour taste in the back of Ben's mouth. His heart was beating wildly, arrhythmically it seemed. Why had he insisted on going after the leopard? He should have given the shotgun to Stuart and sent him up to the cave. It *was* Stuart's leopard. Stuart *had* wounded it. Then it was logical that Stuart should be the one to do this dirty, dangerous work. Ben despised himself. And he was afraid that his childish rivalry with the Texan, their macho *mano a mano*, had escalated to the point now where it just might kill him.

He climbed the last few feet to the base of the wall. It rose vertically until finally vanishing into the clouds. There were a few feet of clear space between the rock and the fringe of brush—not much room, but it seemed a lot in comparison to the claustrophobic forest below.

He moved crabwise along the cliff, his shotgun ready. The cave was about fifty feet away now, around a bulge in the rock. He tried to remember its details; it was shallow, yes, no more than fifteen feet deep, more a hollow created by the overhanging rock than an actual cave. The half-moon-shaped entrance was fairly large, about ten feet wide and six feet high at the center, but it narrowed rapidly, the ceiling sloping down and the walls angling in to form a rough triangle.

The tension was affecting his vision. He paused to blink several times, went on. Jesus, this was hard. He had never done anything that was harder.

Down and to his left, in the woods, he could see a patch of color: Stuart.

He crept slowly around the bulge in the rock. There was the cave entrance. The cat tracks led up through the snow and into the cave. He was in there.

Now Ben moved away from the wall, crouched, aimed the shotgun and hoarsely shouted, "Hey!"

There was a hissing sound inside the cave, another, a moment of silence, and then a soft snarl.

Ben waited. Sweat burned his eyes. His throat was tight, he felt as though he were choking. The shotgun, held tightly and leveled toward the cave opening, was beginning to tire his arms. He waited. The cat was not ready to come out.

Ben slowly removed his left hand from the shotgun and reached into his coat pocket, withdrew a cartridge, and tossed it into the cave. He shouted again, and started backing away to give himself a little more room, a little more time.

He had moved back a few steps and then felt himself slipping on the snow, falling. And at the same instant he saw a tawny blur emerging from the cage. Teeth, slitted eyes, a hissing. But he was out of control, falling backward. There were two quick explosions; the shotgun kicked against his shoulder. Then he was on his back. The shotgun was lost. He twisted quickly and lifted his head—the cat was gone. It hadn't come for him. A moment later he heard the deep crack of Stuart's rifle, followed by a series of diminishing echoes. Silence then.

He got up and brushed the snow off of his clothes. He had hurt his left hip in the fall. And his shoulder was sore from the shotgun's recoil.

Now he could hear the dog barking furiously, without panic. And Stuart was calling to him, but he couldn't understand the words. There was triumph in his voice, though. Both Stuart and the hound bitch were telling the same story. The leopard was dead. Thank God. Ben was glad that the cat had been killed, that it was over at last, and he would not have to endure any more fear and discomfort. He felt an enormous sense of relief. Okay, Stuart had won this phase of their competition. It was over and no one had been hurt. Let the son of a bitch gloat.

Ben picked up his shotgun, broke open the action and blew snow out of the barrels. He could smell and taste the acrid gunpowder. A piece of his upper lip froze to the breach and when he pulled away he could taste blood, too. He cursed. *I had that cat, I had him dead.*

"Hey, Ben! You okay?"

"Coming," he shouted. He inserted two shells into the chambers, closed the shotgun, and started down through the trees. The leopard had leaped about ten feet when the shotgun discharged, headed straight downhill toward Stuart, then suddenly jogged right and begun zigzagging through the brush. And here a great splash of blood. The leopard had gone down, rolled, risen and gone on. Blood all over the snow. Pink, frothy blood—probably a lung shot. He had fallen twice more within the next seventy yards, before running out of blood, out of life.

Stuart was leaning against a tree. The dog was licking a patch of blood-soaked snow.

"Oh, Christ," Ben said.

A small dun-colored mountain lion was half buried in the snow.

"I didn't have time to judge," Stuart said. "I just let go, I couldn't do anything else."

"I know."

"Skinny thing, ain't he? Ribs sticking out, can't weigh eighty pounds. He probably wouldn't have made it through the winter."

"No," Ben said.

"He must be the same mountain lion we ended up tracking yesterday afternoon."

"He has to be."

"That goddamned dog did it to us again."

Ben shook his head. "I can't believe this," he said. "I really can't."

"What kind of dog is it that can't stay on track? She'll be chasing rabbits next."

"I don't know. She knows we're hunting cats. This is a cat. There can't be much scent in all this snow."

"Look at her licking up the bloody snow like it was some kind of flavored snow-cone. That's some dog, Ben."

"Bad luck. Just bad luck, that's all."

"That dog isn't good for anything but stealing pork chops off the dinner table and farting in front of the fire."

"How many dogs do you know of that wouldn't switch off to a hot trail?"

"We trusted her and we should have known better. We should have been more careful, Ben. We knew there was another cat around here somewhere."

"The snow's too deep to tell one cat track from another—they're mostly just holes in the snow."

"Yeah, Ben, but the leopard's bleeding. We should have been looking for blood."

"We should have done a lot of things."

"It's going to be a job now, picking up fresh track."

Ben nodded. "Well, Christ. I don't know. Do you want to take a break now?"

"Naw, Ben, I can walk on these stumps okay. And I don't mind that my clothes got wet and then froze so that I sound like wind chimes when I walk. My ears are going to drop off. Christ, yes, I want to take a break!"

Ben looked at him. "You don't sound quite as cocky as you did this morning."

"I'm not showing much white around my eyes, am I?"

"Not yet."

"Well, there were times today when I worried that your eyes would roll up into your skull and stick there."

"Crap," Ben said.

"Didn't know who was more nervous, you or the dog," Stuart said, cheerful again.

"Let's go back to the cave. We can sit out of the snow, anyway."

"What'll we do with this?" Stuart asked, pressing the toe of his boot against the dead mountain lion.

"Leave him, I guess. Let the dog gnaw on him. I don't care."

They walked back to the cave. Stuart paused outside and studied the tracks. He saw where Ben had stumbled backward for a few steps before falling down; and then he looked up at the rock wall, which had been scarred white by some of the shotgun pellets. He shook his head, glanced sideways at Ben, but did not speak.

They sat down on dry rock beneath the overhang. Stuart removed his left boot and stocking and began roughly massaging his toes.

Ben lit a cigarette. "Do you want to eat?"

"What have you got?"

"A can of pork and beans. We can eat them cold."

"I'm hungry, but not that hungry."

Ben smoked and watched the snow falling past the cave entrance. "I don't know," he said. "This snow . . ."

"Maybe it'll stop soon."

"It doesn't look like it will. Not soon, anyhow. Not before the tracks are covered."

"If the leopard's still around here, and if he's moving, we'll pick up his tracks."

"I don't think we're going to find that leopard today, Stuart. He knows where we are all the time, he can hear us crashing around in the brush, but we haven't got any notion of where he might be. Now this snow—I say we give it up."

"Ben, I don't know that I've ever been more miserable than now, but I'd like to keep hunting for another couple hours."

"How are the feet?"

"This one is starting to hurt."

"Look, you don't want to get frostbite. We really ought to go down now. We can come back up here tomorrow."

"You aren't a real hunter, Ben. You haven't got the patience. Why, once up in Alaska I hunted Dall sheep for nine days. Nine days, half of them in bad weather, but I finally got my trophy head. It's listed in Boone and Crocket."

"What did you kill it with? Hot air?"

"Nope, a rifle, this rifle. And I didn't even fall flat on my ass while pulling the trigger."

"Nice going."

"And I didn't fall down while shooting that little mountain lion, either. In fact, I made a fairly tough shot."

"That cat did everything but run up your rifle barrel."

"Not so. You saw his tracks, he veered off into the heavy woods. He wasn't very far off, but he was moving fast, and he was flashing in and out of the trees. I didn't have time for anything but a snap shot."

Stuart pulled on his stocking and boot. "That foot feels like it's stuck with about a thousand hot needles now." He removed his other boot and stocking and began rubbing the toes.

"You got to show my boy Peter that trick when we get back down," Stuart drawled. "The one where you quick flip over onto your back and shoot holes into the clouds."

"Be glad to," Ben said.

"Tell you one thing, if that leopard is smart he won't be airborne when he comes near you, Ben. You are simply pure death on low-flying cats."

Ben was quiet.

"If they happen to be flying, you'll drop them. Yessir, Ben, you'll pluck those furry yowling devils right out of the sky."

"Just keep it up, Stuart."

"I can't wait to tell my poker buddies about this. 'Damn, boys!' I'll say. 'I got a friend up in New Mexico, a crazy bastard by the name of Ben, who lures wild cats down to treetop level and then shoots them while he's in the middle of a backward somersault. You've never seen anything like it.' "

Against his will, Ben smiled. "Be sure to tell them about your Robin Hood number."

Stuart grinned. "Good to see you smile finally, Ben. You've been a grim companion so far today."

"I suppose."

Stuart pulled on his stocking. "Okay," he said, "let's go see about that pussycat."

"We'll give it another two hours," Ben said.

"Maybe a little longer?"

"Two more hours is plenty for today."

Stuart pulled on his boot. "Patience and fortitude, Ben. Patience and fortitude."

They went back out into the storm. Ben whistled for the dog.

"God," Stuart said. "Isn't this awful, Ben? Isn't it fine? I feel like a kid."

Ninety minutes later they heard a remote thumping and rumbling noise coming from the southwest. It sounded like the rhythmic thunder of an approaching railroad train. The noise gradually increased in volume and proximity, was echoed off the surrounding cliffs; and then suddenly all of the trees swayed, branches clattering and streaming misty clouds of snow. Snow was ripped off the ground and swirled away. Then there was a lull, a period of nearly total silence, before the wind returned, blowing less hard now, but steadily. Falling snowflakes streamed horizontally in the wind. The ground smoked.

Ben knew that it was foolish to continue now, there was no way they could track down the leopard in this blizzard, but he decided to stay out for another hour or two. He intended to punish Stuart. He would teach the big man something about patience and fortitude.

Twenty

Bernard chanted the Origin Song as he gathered wood for the fire. He intended to remain in camp until he heard rifle shots. You could hear gunfire for many miles up here in the high country.

Singing quietly, comforted by the sounds of his own language, he carried some branches across the creek and spread them on the coals.

That Ben, that damn Ben. His face bulged, turned dark when he got mad, and twisted purple veins swelled up on his neck and forehead. His eyes turned pink with blood. That mean Ben.

"Go to hell, Ben," Bernard said aloud.

Ben, he had to name everything. There wasn't anything that he wouldn't name. He was prouder than any Apache. He was even meaner than other white men.

He's my son, my father, my brother, but he's angry and he names things. He buried his father like he was planting squash. Just threw him into a hole in the ground. Ben doesn't know that I dug up the old man that night. I wrapped him in my good Pendleton blanket. I left him my .30-30 rifle and some bullets, a round loaf of bread, chilies and corn, and some horse hairs. I burned the box. I shoveled dirt on the old man and I sang the Song of the Mountains, the Origin Song, the Song of Rain, the Deer Song, and the Song with No Name. And then the old man came out of the ground, turned into an owl, and flew to the moon. His spirit would have been trapped in the box if I hadn't done all those things. But that Benny—no food, no weapons, no songs, not even a prayer. Trap his father's soul in a box and put it into the ground. The coyotes out on the desert saw the owl flying and they howled; they knew that an enemy was gone, and they honored him. I watched the bird fly all the way to the moon. A week later I found a wallet with ninety dollars in it on the town plaza. I bought some eagle feathers from Joseph with the ninety dollars, traded the feathers for an old truck, traded the truck for a horse—but then my nephew shot an owl and the horse got sick and died.

Bernard went out to gather more wood.

That damn Ben. Acting crazy this morning, swearing and yelling, crazy. Ben was a strong man but he relied too much on his strength: he tried to break things, crush them, and then walk over the top. He didn't know how to go around. When things refused to break he got a little crazy. You can't get the leopard with your anger and muscles. Is Ben stronger than the leopard? No. Is Ben angrier than the leopard? No. Is Ben faster than the leopard? No. Is Ben more cunning than the leopard? No. A man must ask for help. You pray first, you sing and you pray, you ask for the right and the power, and if they are denied you go home and wait. You don't try to break through things. You don't name the nameless. You don't plant your father in the ground like squash seeds.

All of Bernard's joints, especially his hips, shoulders, and knuckles, ached from the cold. And he had strained something inside himself yesterday—there was a hot pain low in his belly. Old, yes, he was old.

He carried the wood back to the fire and then opened the rucksack, looking for food and coffee. Whiskey! That damn Ben. Bernard lifted out the three-quarters-full bottle of brandy. His joints ached, the pain made it impossible for him to think clearly, the pain divided him. He would have one swallow for his pain, no more.

He twisted off the cap, tilted the bottle, and drank. It tasted raw, hot, cutting. He liked sweet wines, Tokay, sherry, port, and orange-flavored vodka. His joints hurt, his stomach hurt. He felt divided, as he had during the big war. The whiskey would return him to himself and give him a warm, holy feeling. Everything would become simple again. He would believe.

Bernard drank again. The brandy was warming him, soothing his arthritic pain, lifting him into mystery. He began to feel powerful. He reached into his jacket pocket and withdrew a fang and claw of the spotted cat, the jaguar. He had cut them out while skinning the cat. (No one would know; no one wanted that skin, it had been ruined by the shotgun blasts.) Bits of blood and tissue still clung to the roots. Both the fang and claw were beautifully curved and tapered, one grayish-black and the other white. The cat's magic was his magic. Later he would sing and dance for the spotted cat.

Bernard drank again. He felt that he was slipping in and out of himself. At moments his concentration was so totally focused that he lost self-awareness. It was as though his everyday mind had to be sacrificed in order to achieve this acuity of perception. He had to abandon his mind to free his body. Then he had to discard his body to liberate his soul. His senses broke loose, became diffused; it seemed to him that he could taste and smell and feel the texture of the tree bark as well as see it. He knew other things in the same way. The objects that he observed with such intensity were somehow incorporated into himself. And he was in turn absorbed by the objects. They possessed each other. He could detect the essential harmony between diverse objects. The trees, the land, the snowy earth, the sky became extensions of himself—they were a fractured entity.

Bernard knew that it was now time to dance. He carefully capped the bottle of brandy and moved out into the clearing. He started to chant the Song of the Mountain, but his foot slipped on the snow and he fell heavily on his right hip. The pain dimmed his vision. He heard himself making a low humming sound. He slowly rose to his hands and knees and crawled back to the fire.

His concentration was gone. He was himself again,

old, aching, slow. His senses fogged. The illusion of harmony vanished. There was no more unity between object and object; space cracked them apart, isolated them, opposed one against all the others. The world fragmented, and he was familiarly overwhelmed by stimuli. He felt the heart kick in his chest, pause, kick again, and he almost fainted with the terrible ecstasy of annihilation.

Bernard sat on the snow and rearranged his blanket, wrapping it tightly around his upper body and forming the hood opening into a narrow horizontal slit which exposed only his eyes to the weather. He took another drink from the bottle and then crawled into the lean-to. He was tired and in pain. He needed rest.

When he awakened it was snowing and a hard gusty wind ballooned the lean-to, tautened the fabric, made it snap along the edges with a sound like popping corn. The fire was dead, no heat remained, and snow had drifted over the ashes. He had slept for hours, then. It was afternoon. Perhaps Ben and the big man had already killed the leopard and returned to the house.

He crawled out of the shelter and slowly, testing his sore joints and muscles, rose to his feet. He was still a little drunk. He picked up the bottle of brandy and his shotgun (he would return tomorrow or the next day and collect the rest of the things) and started down the creek, following the three sets of now half-buried tracks: Ben's, the big man's, and the leopard's. He walked gingerly, afraid of falling again.

Down the trail he saw where the dog had joined Ben and the Texan; and farther, where the cat had leaped the creek and headed off toward the cliff country. Here the dog had lain in the snow; Ben had sat on this log; the Texan had walked down to the creek.

Bernard drank from the bottle and then went downstream until he found the place where Ben, the Texan, and the dog had crossed over. He followed their tracks back uphill to the point where they rejoined the leopard's prints and then turned north.

He had another swallow of brandy and cut off into the forest. The alcohol was making him angry. Ben had said that this was government land. It wasn't, it never had been. And down below was the land that Ben called "my ranch." And over there was Indian land. Government land, private land, Indian land— they sliced the land up into little patches, divided it with invisible lines, and said, "This is my land, this is his land, this is your land." Can someone own the earth? They say the earth is just a ball in the sky. Can someone own it? For how long? They divide the water in the streams: "This gallon of water is mine, this gallon is his, this gallon is yours." Who made the water? Did the courts make the water? Who owns the clouds that produce the water? They say: "This deer belongs to the state, you can't shoot it." Then the deer crosses one of their invisible lines and they say: "This deer is on Indian land, you can shoot it now." Did they make the deer? Who made the deer? Did the Spanish and Anglos in the legislature down in Santa Fe make the deer? No, they invented the lines and then they put up fences so you can see the lines. If your horse sticks his head through the wires and eats, they say: "Your horse is eating his grass." Why don't they tell the horse? Why don't they explain it to the grass? If you catch a fish in the wrong place they say: "That's my fish, your fish live over there." The fish don't know anything about lines. Did the fish make the lines? Who are these people who are always making invisible lines? Everything was good and then they came here and started drawing lines on paper. And they named things. The Spanish came and changed the names of all the waters. The People had already named the water a long time ago. And then the whites came and changed the names of the mountains. The People had already named everything that should be named. The others named things all over again and believed they were theirs. They pretend they don't understand the power of names, but they do; they possess with names, words, lines on maps. They're crazy. It's crazy to draw lines on pieces of paper and then say that the paper itself is ground, grass, trees, rain, rabbits, flies, fish, rocks. What's the matter with them? But they go too far; they name things that shouldn't be named, they draw pictures of things and people, trap them, they won't let anything be free. They make invisible lines everywhere, even in time—years, months, weeks, days, hours, minutes, seconds. Do they really see such things?

And if you make a mistake, if you don't understand their invisible lines or the papers with all the words, they'll take your money or your truck, or they'll lock you up in a cage.

So now the People have learned to make lines. Now we say: "This is my tree, my fish, my deer, my corn, my water, stay away." And they don't like it, no.

Someday they'll be gone. We can wait. Someday the People will be alone to practice the old ways. And all the mountains and rivers and valleys and animals will know their names again.

Bernard was confused. It seemed that he had been wandering around this forest for hours, occasionally alert, but sort of sleepwalking most of the time, slipping in and out of himself. He had stopped often to rest and drink brandy, and at one of the stops he had lost his shotgun. It wasn't really lost; it was back there somewhere and he could find it easily enough tomorrow. And he had lost the trail, too. He didn't know when or how that had happened, but the snow around him was untracked, or maybe it was just that the tracks had been covered with snow. The leopard was around here. And so was Ben. He had to find Ben.

Now he was aware that the wind had increased; it thumped and hummed through the tops of the trees, and everywhere the ground and air smoked with blowing snow.

He went on for a few more yards and then slipped and fell down. There was no pain. The snow was soft, comfortable. It seemed that he might have slept for a few minutes.

He could not get his arms and legs untangled. He moved around, trying to reach a position from which it would be easy to arise, but each position was more awkward than the last. It was so simple to stand up except when you had to think about how it was done. Each limb seemed to cancel the effort of the opposite limb; he was just squirming around in the cold snow. His helplessness frightened him.

"Ben!" he cried. "Ben, I'm here, help me!"

He saw the bottle lying on its side in the snow, noticed that there was still a little brandy in it. He locked his hands around the thickest part, lifted it, and drank.

He heard something. Benny? No, it was the wind.

Bernard dropped the bottle and, refusing to think about how to accomplish it, rose to his feet. He staggered over and leaned against a tree. Bowed his head. Vomited.

It was cold, so terribly cold in this wind. He could not feel his feet or hands. He had to get away from here, find Ben, Ben would help him.

He pushed away from the tree, fell down, got up, staggered off into the blowing snow. It was like going down a steep hill when you were tired: you went this way and that, too fast, and then you fell down.

He slowly got up, spread his legs for balance, and then resumed walking, but his torso moved slightly faster than his legs, and he had to move his legs faster and faster to compensate, but then finally his heavier upper body won the race and he sprawled facedown in the snow.

Ben, I can't do it.

He rested for a while and then began crawling on his hands and knees. No, it was too hard, too much for an old man. He collapsed in the snow.

He drowsed; his mind wandered back through the summers of his youth. He had a horse, a rifle, a girl, money in his jeans. He smelled pine, listened to a river, tracked a deer, sweated in the hot sun. He belonged to everything and it all belonged to him. He was drunk and holy without whiskey. He caught a trout with a grass snare. It was warm, he laughed, he teased the girls. The clouds blessed him. It rained. He won foot races. He ate bread hot from the oven, and chilies, and corn. There was no time except the slow ticking of his heart. He prayed. It was night, raining stars, moonlight walked along the riffles of the river.

His body convulsed, and he vomited again. He rolled over onto his back, coughed, spit, cleared his throat.

And then he could feel the leopard's blood-scented breath warming his face, taste blood on the leopard's rough tongue. "Crawl inside me where it's warm," the leopard said in Tewa.

Twenty-one

Ben's concentration was gone. He was cold and hungry and tired, half sick with fatigue (he knew he'd damn sure get a bad cold or the flu out of these past thirty-six hours); and the acute, skin-prickling strain of hunting the cat hour after hour had further dulled his thoughts and reflexes. You could concentrate at that intense a level for only so long before there was a letdown. Now he only wanted to escape his misery, end this futile wandering through a blizzard, get down out of the mountains and back to the house—warmth, a hot meal, a drink, relaxation. There was no chance of getting close to the leopard without a pack of good lion dogs and a break in the weather.

Ben stopped. "You okay?" he asked Stuart.

Stuart nodded.

"We'll give it another three hours and then go down."

"Whatever you say, Ben."

Ben grinned. "You look Christ-awful, a frozen zombie."

"I can go on as long as you can."

"Well, we're going down now."

"Good. I'm for it. I'll keep hunting if you like, but I'd rather get out of here."

"That leopard is holed up somewhere."

"I surely hope he is, Ben, because I can't see or hear much in this storm."

"We'll head straight out to the creek and then down."

"I'll be walking on your heels."

It would be all downhill once they reached the creek, easy going. Say thirty minutes from here to the creek and another forty-five minutes down to the truck, a ten-minute ride to the house—an hour and twenty-five minutes, no more. And they could cut ten or fifteen minutes off that time if they really hurried on the downhill stretch. Misery was endurable if you could calculate exactly when it would end. Anita would have something hot in the oven and on the burners, a pot of good chili probably, that big pork roast, mashed potatoes and gravy, and hot biscuits with butter and honey, peas and carrots. And hot coffee. Jesus. Fires going in every fireplace. Let the dog in—she'd worked hard today, she was suffering—and let her steam and stink in front of a fire.

They went on for about fifteen minutes, taking the easiest route through the brush and trees, and then Ben noticed that the dog was behaving strangely.

"Stay close," Ben yelled over his shoulder.

"What?"

"Move up!"

Now the dog stopped and lifted her muzzle.

"Look out," Ben said.

"What is it, Ben?"

The hound moved her head from side to side, eyes nearly closed; and then the fur along her spine bristled and she backed against Ben's leg.

"I think the leopard's in here somewhere," Ben said.

"Where?" Stuart had moved up and now stood only a few yards behind Ben.

The dog lowered her hindquarters as if to defecate, whined and frantically sniffed the air, and pressed more firmly against Ben's leg.

"He's here," Ben said.

"Where, Ben?"

"Christ, I think he's going to come for us."

"Where *is* he, Ben?"

"I don't know, but he's going to come."

"Oh, shit. *Where is he, Ben?*"

"He's moving, I think he's moving. The dog acts like he's moving around."

"Ben, I can't see anything."

"Keep looking."

"Are there any tracks?"

"No."

"Maybe the dog's spooked on something else."

"Oh, Jesus, I think I can smell the cat."

"Upwind then, he's upwind?"

"I can smell him."

"Where the fuck is he, Ben?"

"I don't *know*!"

"Let's get moving, it's thick in here, we can't see, can't hear in this wind."

"No, stay! We've got to be ready and waiting for him or—"

The dog suddenly bolted forward.

"Behind us!" Ben screamed. He spun around.

The leopard was a swift blur of mottled yellow light against the snow.

Stuart reacted beautifully: he pivoted on his left leg, planted his feet about eighteen inches apart, and shouldered his rifle.

The leopard levitated, effortlessly soared.

Stuart, fast but not fast enough, had assumed the classic rifleman's position.

It happened too quickly, it was a clash of colors and forms; Ben was not able to break the action down into its separate components until much later. He had to think about it, see it happening again and again, dream it, until finally only the essential details remained and it became clear.

The leopard swatted the rifle aside in midair (there was an explosion, the rifle discharged) and seemed to embrace Stuart. They were head to head. Stuart staggered back a few paces, regained his balance, and then moved forward. It looked like a dance. They appeared to kiss. Stuart was trying to get his revolver out of the holster. The leopard was biting Stuart's face and at the same time pumping his hind legs, raking the big man's middle. Neither of them made a sound. It all seemed to be happening at abnormal speed.

And then Stuart was falling and the leopard leaped

aside, dropping lightly into the snow, immediately crouched for another attack. The fur around the cat's jaws was bloody. There was a filmy pink froth of blood on his long, curved canine teeth.

Numb, not thinking, Ben aimed his shotgun. The cat came then, so fast that even though Ben reacted immediately, instinctively, he was almost too slow. The leopard was rising off the ground when he jerked both triggers. The charge took the cat full in the chest, blew him back and to one side.

The leopard lay sprawled out on the blood-splashed snow. He was dead—he had to be dead—but Ben hurriedly reloaded his gun and shot the animal twice more.

Stuart was unconscious. He had deep, blood-welling puncture wounds on his face and head. The animal's canine teeth had pierced his left temple, torn out an eye, and apparently crushed his right cheek-bone.

Ben turned away, walked a few paces. He could not think. Fractured skull. What do you do? Oh, shit, this was something, this was really something.

He returned and kneeled in the snow. Stuart's coat and trousers were slashed and bloody. Ben unzipped the coat and opened it, unbuttoned the shirt. Deep, bloody, ugly wounds. There were more of the same kind of wounds on Stuart's thighs and groin. He was breathing very rapidly and shallowly. His lips were bluish.

Ben scrubbed his hands in the snow, dried them on his thighs, and lit a cigarette. He felt numb, sleepy—he felt as though he could stretch out in the snow and sleep for ten hours. "I can't believe this," he said. Stuart still looked big, massive, but death had shrunk the leopard; the cat appeared much too small to have caused so much harm to that enormous man in so short a time. The cat had just torn him up. Four or five seconds, no more.

Ben lit another cigarette from the butt of the last. Blood all over the snow, everywhere, brilliant red against the white. Blood and snow and wind and cold.

"Jesus," he said. "I can't believe this."

He couldn't think of anything he could do to help Stuart. The Texan was going to die. Maybe he was dead now. Ben looked at him: no, he was still breathing.

"Oh, what a fuck-up," Ben said. His mouth tasted dry, sour. His hands were shaking. There was nothing he could do.

He believed he had seen the cat move. He turned quickly, terrified. No. Impossible.

Well, okay. Think. Got to stay here with Stuart until he dies. Not long. I have to stay with him until he's dead—I don't know why, but it sounds right. Then go down and notify the sheriff and maybe the fire department's rescue team. Lead them back up here and show them where the meat is.

"Robin Hood, huh, Stuart?" Ben said furiously.

Oh, God. Got to tell the woman and the kid. Baptists—I'll take the truck directly to town, notify the cops, pick up the Baptist minister at his house, and take him with me to see Meredith and Peter. He'll know how to handle this kind of thing.

Cash Stuart's checks early tomorrow morning, get the money before all his assets are frozen pending execution of the will. I'll need that money. I earned it fair and square.

Ben kneeled in the snow and looked at Stuart. "Sorry, Tom," he said. "We blew it. Sorry.

"I warned you about that cat!" Ben said, suddenly furious again. "I warned you, you dumb son of a bitch!" He got to his feet.

The cat had really done a job on the big man: punched half a dozen holes in his head and halfway gutted him. In how long? Four or five seconds? And he almost got me, Ben thought. If I had been a microsecond slower I'd be lying in the snow, too.

The dog hesitantly moved out of the trees. The fur along her spine was erect. She was growling softly. She moved in, delicately lifting each paw out of the snow, prepared to flee. She approached, backed away, came forward again, and grabbed the leopard at the throat and began biting and twisting.

"Not *now*!" Ben shouted. He leaped forward and kicked at the dog, missing, almost falling down. "Not now, you goddamned ... you ... you ..." The hound yelped, retreated, sat in the snow and looked mournfully at him. "... You shit eater!"

How can you figure that cat? He ran from us all day, ran, circled, hid, didn't let us see a piece of him the size of a dime. And then when we're going, leaving him behind, not hunting him anymore, he ambushes us. *He* comes for *us*! Terrific cat, wild, vindictive as hell, cold, a great animal.

Ben kneeled in the snow again. "Tom?" Stuart's eyes had opened halfway and the fluids were dull and sticky-looking. No sign of respiration. Ben couldn't find a pulse. Stuart was dead then, or so close to death that only the angels knew for sure. "Sorry," Ben muttered. "Sorry, guy."

Ben and the dog were walking directly south, toward the creek, when suddenly the dog stopped and lifted her muzzle, smelling the wind. Then she barked once and, tail high, eagerly ran off into the brush. Ben could see that she was not after game, but was going off to greet a friend. Bernard, of course. The Indian had heard the shotgun blasts and was coming to skin out the leopard. Wait until Bernard hears about this, Ben thought, hurrying after the dog.

Bernard was lying in the snow less than seventy-five yards away. The dog found him.

Bernard was alive. He stank of alcohol and vomit, but was breathing steadily.

"I ought to leave you here," Ben said.

He removed Bernard's mittens. The Indian's hands were cold and mottled white down to the second knuckles, but there did not appear to be any serious frostbite. His toes were white, too, and cold and hard.

Ben replaced Bernard's boots and mittens. It would take too long to build a fire here—the wood was wet, the wind was blowing half a gale; the thing was to get him down to the house and throw him into a bathtub of warm water. Thaw out the old piece of shit, take him to the hospital afterward if it seemed necessary.

Ben cuffed him on the side of his head. Again, not so lightly. "Can you hear me?" Slapped him again.

Bernard opened his eyes, tried to focus them.

"Can you understand what I'm saying?"

"Ho, Ben," he said in a thick voice.

"Can you walk, Bernard, or do I have to carry your sorry ass down out of here?"

Bernard closed his eyes.

Ben slapped him again. "You stink, Bernard. You puked all over yourself. I think you must have crapped your pants, too. I'd rather not have to carry anything that stinks as much as you do at this particular moment."

"Can't walk, Ben."

"Paralyzed yourself, huh? That's smart."

"No legs, Ben."

"No brain."

"Brain gone, Ben."

Ben laughed.

"Old, Ben, old. Old. Too old, much too old, you know?"

"Naw, Bernard, you're not too old. Tom Stuart's too old. You and me, we're just babes."

THE BEST OF FORGE

☐ 53441-7   CAT ON A BLUE MONDAY $4.99
       Carole Nelson Douglas   Canada $5.99

☐ 53538-3   CITY OF WIDOWS $4.99
       Loren Estleman   Canada $5.99

☐ 51092-5   THE CUTTING HOURS $4.99
       Julia Grice   Canada $5.99

☐ 55043-9   FALSE PROMISES $5.99
       Ralph Arnote   Canada $6.99

☐ 52074-2   GRASS KINGDOM $5.99
       Jory Sherman   Canada $6.99

☐ 51703-2   IRENE'S LAST WALTZ $4.99
       Carole Nelson Douglas   Canada $5.99

Buy them at your local bookstore or use this handy coupon:
Clip and mail this page with your order.

Publishers Book and Audio Mailing Service
P.O. Box 120159, Staten Island, NY 10312–0004

Please send me the book(s) I have checked above. I am enclosing $ _____
(Please add $1.25 for the first book, and $.25 for each additional book to cover postage and handling. Send check or money order only—no CODs.)

Name _____
Address _____
City _____ State / Zip _____
Please allow six weeks for delivery. Prices subject to change without notice.

THE BEST OF FORGE

☐ 55052-8	LITERARY REFLECTIONS *James Michener*	Canada	$5.99 $6.99
☐ 52046-7	A MEMBER OF THE FAMILY *Nick Vasile*	Canada	$5.99 $6.99
☐ 55056-0	MY UNFORGETTABLE SEASON—1970 *Red Holzman*	Canada	$4.99 $5.99
☐ 58193-8	PATH OF THE SUN *Al Dempsey*	Canada	$4.99 $5.99
☐ 51380-0	WHEN SHE WAS BAD *Ron Faust*	Canada	$5.99 $6.99
☐ 52145-5	ZERO COUPON *Paul Erdman*	Canada	$5.99 $6.99

Buy them at your local bookstore or use this handy coupon:
Clip and mail this page with your order.

Publishers Book and Audio Mailing Service
P.O. Box 120159, Staten Island, NY 10312–0004

Please send me the book(s) I have checked above. I am enclosing $ _____
(Please add $1.25 for the first book, and $.25 for each additional book to cover postage and handling. Send check or money order only—no CODs.)

Name _____
Address _____
City _____ State / Zip _____
Please allow six weeks for delivery. Prices subject to change without notice.

WESTERN ADVENTURE
FROM TOR

☐	58459-7	THE BAREFOOT BRIGADE *Douglas Jones*	$4.95 Canada $5.95
☐	52303-2	THE GOLDEN SPURS *Western Writers of America*	$4.99 Canada $5.99
☐	51315-0	HELL AND HOT LEAD/GUN RIDER *Norman A. Fox*	$3.50 Canada $4.50
☐	51169-7	HORNE'S LAW *Jory Sherman*	$3.50 Canada $4.50
☐	58875-4	THE MEDICINE HORN *Jory Sherman*	$3.99 Canada $4.99
☐	58329-9	NEW FRONTIERS I *Martin H. Greenberg & Bill Pronzini*	$4.50 Canada $5.50
☐	58331-0	NEW FRONTIERS II *Martin H. Greenberg & Bill Pronzini*	$4.50 Canada $5.50
☐	52461-6	THE SNOWBLIND MOON *John Byrne Cooke*	$5.99 Canada $6.99
☐	58184-9	WHAT LAW THERE WAS *Al Dempsey*	$3.99 Canada $4.99